The Michigan
Mega-Monsters

Other books by Johnathan Rand:

#1: The Michigan Mega-Monsters

Johnathan Rand

An AudioCraft Publishing, Inc. book

Book storage and warehouses provided by Chillermania!©
Indian River, Michigan

Warehouse security provided by:
Lily Munster and Scooby-Boo

American Chillers #1: The Michigan Mega-Monsters
ISBN 13-digit: 978-1-893699-19-9

Librarians/Media Specialists:
PCIP/MARC records available at www.americanchillers.com

Cover illustration by Dwayne Harris
Cover layout and design by Sue Harring

Printed in USA

The Michigan Mega-Monsters

VISIT CHILLERMANIA!

WORLD HEADQUARTERS FOR BOOKS BY JOHNATHAN RAND!

CHILLERMANIA!

**I-75 Exit 313
then south
1 mile!**

Visit the HOME for books by Johnathan Rand! Featuring books, hats, shirts, bookmarks and other cool stuff not available anywhere else in the world! Plus, watch the American Chillers website for news of special events and signings at **CHILLERMANIA!** with author Johnathan Rand! Located in northern lower Michigan, on I-75! Take exit 313 . . . then south 1 mile! For more info, call (231) 238-0338. And be afraid! Be veeeery afraaaaaaiiiid . . . .

1

Summer camp is supposed to be fun. It's supposed to be games and swimming and hot dogs and campfires and silly pranks.

It's *supposed* to be.

But not this year. Not at Camp Willow. What I went through at Camp Willow was one of the most horrifying experiences of my life.

To get to the camp, I rode the bus with a bunch of other kids. It was a long ride. I live in Grand Rapids, and Camp Willow is near Rochester Hills, which is on the other side of the state.

My name was being called just as I was getting off the bus. There was a man with a megaphone, holding it to his mouth and speaking. He was standing with a group of a dozen kids that were about my age. Other buses had arrived, and their passengers were unloading.

"Last call for Rick Owens!" his voice boomed out. "Is there a Rick Owens here?"

"Right here!" I hollered out, slinging my heavy pack over my shoulder.

"Hurry it up! We haven't got all day!"

Jeepers, I thought. *I just got here. Give me a break.*

I joined the group of waiting campers. They were all my age, boys and girls. I didn't recognize any of them.

"Campers! Welcome to Camp Willow!" the man with the megaphone blurted out. "My name is Mr. Leonard, and I'll be your patrol leader. Take a few minutes to make sure you have all of your gear, and then we'll assign you to your cabins."

Camp Willow is really cool. There is a main

lodge and about ten cabins that surround Willow Lake, which is pretty small. In fact, you won't find the camp or the lake on any map. But kids from all over Michigan—even from around the country—come here every year. It's a popular camp, and I'd been waiting all summer.

Of course, that was before everything happened.

Before the Mega-Monsters.

Oh, you can think what you want. But Mega-Monsters exist.

I know. I saw them. So did my friends. And the terror would begin that very first night at camp.

2

My group was called the Wolf Patrol. I was assigned a cabin with five other guys, and we stored our gear and then met for a short patrol meeting around the big fire pit. Mr. Leonard handed out a sheet of rules, and then we all took a few minutes to meet one another in the group.

"I'm Rick Owens," I said to a girl standing to the left of me. "I'm from Grand Rapids."

"I'm Leah," she said. "Leah Warner. I'm from Saginaw." She had a friendly smile, and she was a little taller than me.

A blonde-haired girl in front of us turned around. "I've been to Saginaw," she said, her eyes lighting up. "My family travels through Saginaw when we go north to visit Mackinac Island. My name is Sandy Johnson."

We talked for a few minutes. I liked Leah and Sandy. They were pretty cool. I met some other kids in our patrol that were from other states. One kid came all the way from California!

The rest of the day was spent getting to know our way around the camp. Our patrol leader took us around and showed us different things like where the camp store was, where to go in case of an emergency, and where the mess hall was. The mess hall was a huge room in the main lodge where all of the campers gathered three times a day for meals. Our first meal in the mess hall was going to be at seven o'clock the next morning.

After we were shown around Camp Willow, the rest of the evening was free time. I wandered down by the lake and talked with Leah and Sandy. We were all excited about the things we would be doing during the week. Fishing, hiking, swimming, canoeing . . . this was going to be the best week of the summer!

I had a hard time falling asleep that night. I was so excited. Finally, after counting a billion sheep, I finally fell asleep.

But not for long.

I was awakened by a terrible nightmare. It was *awful.* I dreamed that I was in my cabin and there were big, red eyes glowing in the window! The eyes belonged to a horrible creature, and in my dream I could hear him breathing just outside my window. He was looking at me the way a dog looks at a steak bone.

Suddenly, I awoke and sat straight up in bed. My heart was pounding, and I was breathing heavily. I'm not sure what time it was, but it was really dark. My bunkmates were all sleeping.

I turned to look out the window, afraid of what might be there.

Nothing.

Whew, I thought. *A dream. That's all it was.* I laid back down, and, after a while, I fell back asleep.

Next morning, I was jolted awake by a trumpeting bugle. It was *loud!* There was no way anyone was going to sleep through that!

I showered and dressed and got ready to go to the mess hall for breakfast—but when I walked out the door of the cabin, I got the shock of my life.

There, in the soft earth, were footprints. Not human footprints, but strange, claw-like footprints, much bigger than a human's.

And the footprints led right up to the window by my bed!

3

At the mess hall, I sat with Sandy and Leah. I told them about my dream and about the tracks beneath my window.

"That's pretty freaky," Leah said.

"In your dream, did you see what the creature looked like?" Sandy asked.

"Not really," I said. "It had red eyes, and maybe a big nose. I guess I don't remember anything else, except the fact that it was gross-looking."

"It was probably just someone trying to scare

you, that's all," Leah offered. She took a sip of orange juice and returned the glass to the table. "You know. Just a prank."

I shook my head. "Those footprints didn't look like they were made by a human," I said.

I sat quietly during the rest of breakfast. Sandy and Leah got along well, and they talked a lot to one another. All around me, dozens of kids talked and laughed and ate cereal and French toast. One dark-haired kid at the end of our table was really loud and obnoxious. He threw a strawberry and hit another kid on the other side of the mess hall, then pretended that he hadn't done anything. Every camp has a troublemaker, and it looked like he was going to be the one this week.

But I kept thinking about the creature in my dream. And the footprints.

Leah is right, I told myself. *It was probably someone just playing a prank. A joke. There is no such thing as monsters.*

Our patrol spent the morning hiking and learning the names of all the trees. I even caught a grass snake! Then we all went out in canoes and rowed around the lake. It was a blast! We splashed other kids in our patrol with our paddles, and by the time we were done, all of us were soaked. By lunchtime, I had forgotten all about my dream and the footprints.

Not for long.

Our afternoon activity was swimming. Our patrol, and several other patrols, met down by the beach. The day was hot and there wasn't a cloud in the sky.

Our patrol leader pointed to the buoys. "Nobody goes beyond that point," he ordered. "Stay in the swim area. Everybody understand?"

We all nodded and spoke up, eager to dive into the cool water.

"You've got thirty minutes. When the bell rings, get dried off and meet by the flagpole."

I was the first to hit the water, followed by my fellow members of the Wolf Patrol. The water was cool and fresh. There was a diving board at the end of the dock, and we took turns diving.

I guess Sandy hadn't been paying attention, because when I saw her, she was a few feet beyond the buoys . . . outside of the swim area.

"Sandy!" I called out. She turned her head. "You're outside of the swim area!"

She waved, and then began swimming back toward shore. I turned around to jump off the diving board . . . but in the next instant I was stopped by Sandy's piercing scream. I spun, just in time to see a horrified look on her face.

"SOMETHING'S GOT ME!" she screamed in panic. *"IT'S GOT ME! IT'S GOT MY LEG!"*

Suddenly, she was pulled beneath the surface. Sandy was gone.

I ran down the end of the dock and plunged into the water. A lifeguard was at his post and he, too, dove into the water to help.

All of a sudden, Sandy's head popped above the surface. She was sputtering and coughing.

"Hang on Sandy!" I shouted as I crawled arm over arm through the water.

Just then, another head emerged right next to Sandy. It was the dark-haired kid that threw the strawberry during breakfast.

"Ha ha ha!" he smirked. "Gotcha!"

"Jerk!" Sandy scolded.

"Fooled ya, fooled ya," the kid teased, swimming away.

I reached Sandy. "What happened?" I asked.

"That kid snuck up under me and grabbed my ankle and pulled me under," she said sharply. By now, Leah had swum up to us, and we all headed back to the dock. On shore, the lifeguard was scolding the dark-haired kid. He kicked him out of the water for the rest of the day.

"See?" Leah said smartly as she climbed up the wooden ladder to the dock. "He got what he deserved."

"I'll get him back somehow," Sandy said. She was really angry. "Maybe I'll sneak up to his cabin at night and scare the daylights out of him," she said.

I didn't think that she was serious — until later that night.

Sometime after midnight, I was awakened by screaming coming from the cabin next to mine. The kids had all of the lights on, and the dark-haired troublemaker was standing by the door with a flashlight, screaming something about a monster. That kid was really spooked!

I smiled. *You really got him back, Sandy,* I said, climbing back into bed. *You got him good.*

The next morning, I found Leah and Sandy in the mess hall.

"Nice going!" I said to Sandy as I sat down.

She had a puzzled look on her face. "What do you mean?" she asked.

"Scaring that dark-haired goofball," I replied. "You know . . . last night."

"I didn't do anything," Sandy insisted, shaking her head. "I mean, I would have *liked* to, but I'm not going to do anything that is going to get me in trouble."

"You . . . you mean . . . that wasn't you last night? Scaring that kid?"

"Nope," Sandy assured me, shaking her head again. Her light blonde hair brushed her cheeks. "I was sound asleep."

Terror began to well up inside me. *If it wasn't Sandy playing a joke last night, then what did that kid see? Did he really see something?*

I had to know.

Without saying a word, I got up from the breakfast table and left the mess hall. I ran all the way to the kid's cabin, searching the ground.

It didn't take long.

On the ground, all around the cabin, were footprints—exactly like the ones I'd seen at my cabin yesterday morning!

5

The rumors about the monster began to spread. There were other kids that said they had spotted something, and lots of kids saw the tracks in the soft earth.

Was there really some strange creature stalking the campers? If so, where did it come from?

Our patrol was supposed to go fishing that day, but it started to rain. We gathered in the main lodge and played indoor games. Most of them were kind of boring, and I just kind of hung out and watched.

And thought about the monster that I had seen in my dream.

And the one that the dark-haired goofball had seen.

I decided that I would go and find the kid and talk to him. I knew he was a troublemaker, and I didn't like him . . . but I *had* to know. I *had* to know what he saw.

I couldn't find him in the main lodge, so I went to his cabin. The rain was starting to let up, and it looked like the sun might come out again.

I pounded on the door of the cabin.

"Hello?" I said. "Anybody here?"

No answer.

I pushed on the door, and it swung open.

"Anybody home?" I called out, stepping inside.

The cabin was tidy, but I noticed something odd.

Although there were six beds, only *five* beds had gear piled around. I thought all the cabins were supposed to be full.

I left the cabin and returned to the main lodge.

Mr. Williams, the camp director, was in his office.

"Excuse me," I said, knocking on the open door as I spoke.

"Yes?" he said. He looked up from his pile of papers. "Everything okay?"

"Yes," I replied. "I was just looking for someone. I don't know his name, but he has dark hair and he—"

"He's gone," Mr. Williams said flatly. "Left an hour ago."

"Where did he go?" I asked.

"Home. Got scared. At least that's what I was told. His parents came and picked him up."

Scared? I thought. *He got so scared that he left camp?*

I found Leah and Sandy in the mess hall and told them about the kid leaving.

"Good," said Sandy. "Serves him right. At least we won't have to put up with him for the whole week."

But I wanted to know more. Whatever that kid saw, it scared him bad enough to leave.

And maybe I hadn't had a nightmare, after all. Maybe I really saw something.

That night, around the campfire, I was about to find out.

All of us in Wolf Patrol gathered around our campfire. We roasted marshmallows and were telling jokes. The sun had gone down long ago, and a million stars dotted the sky. Everyone was having fun . . . until a chilling scream pierced the night.

Everyone around the campfire stopped talking. A chill raced down my spine. Not a word was spoken.

And then, we heard the crunching of branches, coming closer and closer.

"Who's there?" Mr. Leonard called out.

"Just me," said a very human, adult voice.

Whew! You could actually feel the relief in the air when we realized it was only one of the camp counselors.

His shadowy form came closer to the fire. When we saw him in the flickering light, our entire group gasped in horror.

From where I sat, it looked like the counselor was covered from head to toe — *in blood.*

6

Mr. Leonard jumped up and rushed over to the man. "Are you okay?" he asked.

"Yeah," the counselor said. "Someone was painting the storage shed, and they left an open can of paint on the ladder. I didn't see it in the dark. I got this stuff all over me!"

Whew! He wasn't covered in blood, after all! It was only red paint!

Some of the kids around the campfire giggled. He *did* look pretty funny, now that we knew he wasn't hurt.

"I've got to go get this stuff washed off," he said.

"Here," Mr. Leonard said, handing him his flashlight. "You can borrow this so you can see where you're going."

The counselor took the light and left, and Mr. Leonard sat back down by the fire.

"Mr. Leonard?" I said. All of the other campers looked at me while I spoke, and their faces glowed orange in the firelight. "What's up with the strange tracks that we've all seen?"

"Yeah," Sandy chimed in. "The bratty kid went home because he was afraid. Everyone says that he saw some creature."

Some of the kids bobbed their heads. They all wanted to know more.

Mr. Leonard looked around at the group huddled around the fire, his eyes meeting with each of our own. "Do you really want to know?" he asked.

We all nodded our heads.

"There is a legend," he began, "about the Michigan Mega-Monsters. They're supposed to come from the swamp on the other side of the lake. No one is exactly sure where they came from. But once in a while, some of the campers here have said they have seen them."

"Have you ever seen one?" Leah asked.

Mr. Leonard paused, took a deep breath, and nodded his head. "Yes, I have," he finally replied.

There were a few quiet gasps from the campers. A girl across from me placed her hand over her mouth. Her face was gripped in shock.

"What do they look like?" I asked Mr. Leonard.

"Well, they're ugly," he replied. "The ugliest things I've ever seen in my life. As tall as me and covered with slime and seaweed. Dark red eyes and long fangs. The legend says that at night, they leave the swamp and wander the woods."

Everyone in our patrol was silent. All we could hear was the crackling fire and the sounds of crickets in the darkness.

"Wh . . . what do they want?" one of the kids stammered.

"No one knows," Mr. Leonard answered, shaking his head. "We've blocked off all of the trails to keep them out, and to keep hikers away from the swamp. But the Mega-Monsters still find their way through the forest."

"I don't believe it," one of the patrol members said. "I don't think there is any such thing as a 'Michigan Mega-Monster'."

"Believe what you want," Mr. Leonard said. "Just stay away from the swamp. Don't ever go near the swamp." His voice was chilling and cold.

I wasn't sure if I believed him or not, either. But who — or what — made those tracks around the cabins? Was it someone playing a joke?

I didn't know it at the time, but very soon, I would find out that the legends of the Michigan Mega-Monsters were true.

And it all started later that night when I was awakened by a terrible scratching on the cabin door.

7

I don't know what time it was when it happened.
The cabin was really dark. I had woken up a
couple times because the kid sleeping in the bunk
next to me was snoring his head off! He sounded
like a lawnmower. I reached over and tapped him
on the shoulder and he stopped. After I went
back to sleep, he started snoring again. I tell you
. . . he snored worse than my dad!

But then I was awakened by something else.
At first, I thought it was the snoring kid. I was
about to tap him on the shoulder again, but a

strange scratching sound caught my attention.

A scratching sound . . . *at the cabin door!*

It was loud, too. It wasn't like a dog or a cat scratching. Whatever was scratching at the door was *big*. The scratching sound even woke up the snoring kid.

"What's that?" he whispered, sitting up in his bunk.

"I don't know," I answered quietly.

By now, other kids in the cabin were awake. I couldn't see them in the darkness, but I heard their bunks squeak as they sat up in bed.

Scraaaaaaaaaatttcchhhhh . . . .

The loud scraping caused us all to shake with fear.

"It might just be one of the counselors playing a joke," someone whispered in the dark.

Just then, a flashlight clicked on in our cabin. A kid got up and turned on a lamp, and the darkness vanished.

Sssscraaaaaaaatch . . . .

There it was again!

The kid with the flashlight leapt back into bed, and the six of us sat staring at the door.

Ssscraaaaaaaatchhhhhh . . . .

I didn't know what to do. The noise sounded awful. It was loud, and it was on the other side of the door.

Whatever it was, it wanted in.

Then: silence. Seconds ticked by. Then minutes.

"Maybe it's gone," I whispered.

"I want my mom," another kid said, his voice trembling in fear.

"It was probably the wind," another kid said.

I shook my head. "That was no wind," I said. "That wasn't the wind at all."

We sat in silence, the six of us, each huddled in our bunks. What was behind the door? What had made the awful scratching sound?

There was only one way to find out.

I pulled back the covers and swung my feet to the floor.

"What are you going to do?" the snoring kid asked.

"I'm going to find out what made that noise," I said, standing up.

"It's a Mega-Monster!" a kid said, ducking

under the sheets. "I know it is! He's hungry, and he's going to eat us all!"

"Are you really going to see what it is?" someone asked me.

"Yes," I said. I tip-toed quietly across the wood floor.

"Let me know when it's over," the kid beneath the covers said. Then he poked his head out from beneath the sheets and looked at me. "If I get eaten," he said, "my mom and dad are going to be really mad at you!" He crawled beneath the covers and trembled.

I was almost at the door. We hadn't heard the scratching sound in a few minutes, and I thought that whatever had made the sound was probably gone.

"Be careful," a voice from behind me called out quietly.

Slowly, ever so slowly, I reached out and grasped the door knob. It made a clunking sound as it turned.

Ka-thunk. The door popped open, and I pulled it toward me. Light from the cabin lit up the outside. All I could see were shadowy trees.

I spoke. "There's no one—"

When I looked at the outside of the door, I stopped speaking. My voice froze. I gasped in horror. The kids in my cabin gasped. What I saw on the door was horrible.

On the outside of the door were huge, deep gashes in the wood.

Claw marks.

They were wide and deep and long. Whatever had made the gashes was big, and very strong.

And on the ground —

Footprints. Like giant claws in the ground. They were just like the ones I'd seen a couple nights ago.

But there was also something more.

Seaweed. Wet, slimy seaweed was scattered

37

about all over the ground near the door and around the cabin.

"What is it?" I heard someone whisper from behind me.

"I don't know," I replied quietly.

But I think I did know. I think I knew what had made the scratches on the door and the footprints, but I was too afraid to admit it.

Do Mega-Monsters really exist? I wondered. I turned around. The five other kids in the cabin were still sitting in their beds.

"Does anyone want to go look for him?" I asked.

"You're crazy!" was all I heard. I think everyone said it at the same time. It didn't look like I was going to get any help from the guys in my cabin.

I turned and looked out the door, and stared into the dark night.

Suddenly, I had an idea.

Sandy and Leah, I thought. *They would help. They would want to search for the creature.*

I got dressed. All the other guys in the cabin thought that I was crazy. I thought they were a bunch of chickens.

But I knew that Sandy and Leah wouldn't be.

I slipped out the cabin door, clicked on my flashlight, walked over to Sandy and Leah's cabin . . . and there was a light on! The cabin door was open, and someone was standing in the yellow glow of the lamp inside.

"Rick? Is that you?" I recognized Leah's voice instantly.

"Yeah," I answered, walking up to the cabin. Just then, Sandy appeared in the door, too.

"I heard a noise," I said. "And I saw —"

" — we did, too," Leah interjected, her head nodding up and down. "Footprints. Look."

She pointed to the ground. The same, claw-like prints were all over the ground around the cabin.

"We were going to go look for it," Sandy said.

"That's why I came," I said. "Let's go look for him together. It would be safer that way."

Sandy and Leah stepped out of the cabin.

"I hope we don't get in trouble," Leah said.

"We won't go far," I said. "And we won't even leave the camp. There are plenty of trails right around here that we can search."

"What if we find some freaky creature?" Sandy asked. "Then what?"

Good question.

"Well," I replied, "then we'll run and get Mr. Leonard."

I led the way down a dark trail, carrying my flashlight. Every few seconds we would stop and listen. We didn't hear anything—at first. But then, Leah grabbed my arm.

"Shhhh!" she whispered. "I think I just heard something."

I turned the flashlight off. The three of us stood on the dark trail, listening. Above us, spiny tree branches wove through a star-clustered sky. Crickets chirped from the shadows.

And when we heard the crunching of branches, I think we all about fell out of our skin. The noise wasn't a long ways off. Whatever was making the noise was only a few feet away, hidden in the dark bushes.

And it was coming right toward us.

We were frozen with fear. The loud crunching in the brush was only a few feet away.

"Turn on the light!" Sandy hissed. "Quick!"

I clicked on my flashlight, and the first thing I saw were the glowing eyes —

of a raccoon!

"Good grief," Leah said. "Some creature-hunters we are. We were scared silly by a little raccoon!"

I think we scared the animal more than he scared us, though. As soon as he saw the flashlight, the raccoon fled in terror, running through the forest. He was gone in an instant.

"Come on," I said. "Let's go look down by the beach. Mr. Leonard said that the Mega-Monsters like water. Maybe we'll see something down there."

We turned around and walked back down the trail, passing by the main lodge and the mess hall where we would be having breakfast in the morning. Then we walked down a steep slope and emerged on the dark, sandy beach.

The moon reflected on the still surface of Willow Lake, and we could still hear a bajillion crickets singing all around us.

I shined the light down into the sand. If anything had been here recently, they would easily make tracks in the soft sand.

We searched and searched. Finally, right by the lake—

A clue.

There were strange footprints in the soft sand near the water! Piles of seaweed were clumped about!

"It was here!" Leah exclaimed. "It really was!

It was right here!"

The tracks wound back up the beach, and we followed them until they reached the forest. I think we were all a little nervous, knowing that at any moment, the creature could come out of the woods and come after us.

Finally, the tracks became too hard to see in the woods, and we decided to go back. We could try again tomorrow during our free time when it would be daylight.

But it didn't look like we were going to have the chance. Because in the moonlight, down by the beach, we suddenly saw a movement. It was big—much bigger than a raccoon.

Sandy, Leah, and I stopped dead in our tracks. We could see the outline of the creature in the moonlight, but my flashlight wasn't bright enough to illuminate the shadow.

But there was no mistake. Whatever the creature was, it was bigger than we were.

And it was coming for us . . . *fast*.

We were frantic.

"We've got to get out of here!" Leah hissed. *"It's going to see us!"*

"I think it already has!" I said.

"Let's run!" Sandy exclaimed.

That sounded like the best idea. We turned to run the other way . . . but we didn't get far.

"Stop!" I heard a voice call out. I turned, and saw a flashlight coming toward us. Man, was I happy to see that! It wasn't a Mega-Monster after all!

"I thought I saw someone out here," the voice said, as the form came closer.

We waited on the trail as the light approached. My heart thumped madly in my chest.

"Uh-oh," I said. "I think we're going to get in trouble."

Sure enough, it was the camp director, Mr. Williams. He walked up to us.

"What are you kids doing out here?" he demanded.

"We thought we saw a Mega-Monster," Sandy replied. "We saw tracks around our cabin."

"And there were scratches on our door," I said.

"There is no such thing as Mega-Monsters," Mr. Williams replied. He glared at us. "You three need to go back to your cabins. You shouldn't be out after dark."

Mr. Wilson followed us as we walked through the camp. He didn't seem like he was really mad, which was good. I thought we were going to get into a lot of trouble for being out after dark.

We arrived at Leah and Sandy's cabin, and they turned and walked to it.

"See you tomorrow," I said as they reached the door.

"Good night," Leah and Sandy said. They disappeared into their cabin.

I continued to my cabin, and I turned around to see Mr. Williams walking back to the main lodge. Again, I was thankful that we hadn't gotten into trouble.

The lights were on in my cabin. When I walked inside, the other guys were still up, waiting for me. They all wanted to know what happened.

"Nothing," I explained. "We got scared by a raccoon and Mr. Williams. We saw some tracks, but we didn't find any Mega-Monsters."

I climbed back into bed, and someone turned off the light.

Tomorrow we'll know, I thought. *Tomorrow we'll hike over to the other side of the lake. Tomorrow we'll know the truth about the Michigan Mega-Monsters.*

Tomorrow.

I closed my eyes and listened to the crickets chirping outside my cabin window.

Tomorrow. We'll find out for sure tomorrow.

It was to be a day that Sandy, Leah, and I would never, ever forget.

11

I was awakened once again by the loud trumpet. It was time for breakfast.

At the mess hall, I met Sandy and Leah and the other members of the Wolf Patrol. While we ate fruit and cereal, Mr. Williams explained what activities we would be doing today. We would have two hours of free time after lunch.

"I don't think I can wait that long," Leah said. "I want to go find that swamp."

"Me too," Sandy agreed.

I couldn't wait, either. I wanted to search for

the Mega-Monsters right away.

The morning activities were fun, at least. We went to the archery range after breakfast, and that was a blast. I'm pretty good with a bow and arrow, and I got the highest score in the patrol.

Then we went back to the mess hall for a first-aid course, and after that we went for a nature walk. Mr. Leonard quizzed us on the names of the trees.

I didn't look at many trees, though. I was too busy looking for Mega-Monster tracks. I found a few animal tracks, but none that looked like they had been made by any Mega-Monsters.

If there really *was* such a thing as a Mega-Monster.

Finally, after lunch, came free time. I met Leah and Sandy down by the beach.

"Ready?" I asked.

"Yep," Sandy replied.

"As ready as we'll ever be," Leah said.

We set out on the trail that wound around the lake. The forest was thick, and we pushed branches out of our way as we plodded down the thin path. Sure enough, we soon found signs that told us to turn back. One sign read:

UNKNOWN TERRITORY AHEAD
TURN BACK NOW

"Anybody want to turn around?" I asked.

Leah and Sandy both shook their heads, and we continued on.

The forest around us grew thicker, and the path became thinner. The sky grew dark, and it looked like it might rain.

"Still want to keep going?" I asked, looking up at the cloudy sky.

"Oh, I don't think you'll melt if it rains," Leah laughed.

We kept going.

Finally, we came to the swamp. It was small, maybe about the size of the parking lot at McDonald's. The swamp was thick with cattails and other plants that grew in the mushy earth.

"No Mega-Monsters here," I said, eyeing the marsh.

But something was very strange.

"This is really weird," Leah said. "I'm not

sure what it is, but there is something wrong with this swamp."

Leah was right, but I just couldn't put my finger on it.

I looked around. Trees grew thick around the swamp, which seemed to be attached to the lake. From where we stood, however, it was impossible to see the water through the dense trees. The sky was very, very dark, and I knew that at any moment it would open up, drenching the three of us in a heavy downpour of rain.

"It sure is quiet," Sandy said, her voice just louder than a whisper.

"That's it!" I said. *"That's what's wrong! There are no sounds at all! Listen!"*

We stood motionless, listening for any sounds from the swamp or trees — but we heard nothing. No birds, no insects. Not even any wind. It was eerie.

"This is really creepy," I said, looking around. "I can't believe that a forest can be this quiet."

And then —

A sound.

It was very faint at first, kind of like a

bubbling sound. I couldn't tell where it was coming from.

"Do you hear that?" I whispered. Sandy and Leah nodded their heads. We listened.

The strange gurgling grew louder. It sounded like it was coming from the swamp, but I couldn't see anything.

Thunder boomed in the distance. The sky looked like it would open up at any moment and dump buckets of rain upon us.

We remained very still.

Watching . . . .

Suddenly, cattails and reeds began to move! In the middle of the swamp, the plants shuddered and shook. The three of us looked on, wondering what it was. Sandy grasped my arm, holding it tightly.

"What is it?" she whispered.

And when the creature appeared, I thought that I was going to fall over in fright.

It was big.

And ugly.

It was a Mega-Monster.

12

There was only one word to describe the creature we saw coming out of the swamp:

Hideous.

It was the grossest thing I had ever seen in my life. The beast was a green-brown color. It looked like it might have had hair, but maybe it was just seaweed. It had huge arms and long, sharp claws. Its nose was big, and was shaped like a pig's snout. Huge red eyes glowed within dark, black sockets.

"Oh my gosh," Sandy whispered. Her voice

trembled as she spoke. *"The legends are true! There really are Mega-Monsters!"*

"Do you think he sees us?" Leah asked.

"I don't think so," I whispered back. *"He's not looking in our direction."*

But I knew it might be only a matter of seconds before we were spotted.

I turned my head slowly, and saw a clump of dense brush a few feet away.

"Come on," I urged. *"Let's hide before he sees us."*

We slipped quickly back and into the bushes, crouching down and ducking out of sight.

In the middle of the swamp, the Mega-Monster was standing up. He was huge! He was bigger than a grownup, and twice as wide. I wondered if it was a good idea to come to the swamp after all.

"Where do you suppose they came from?" Leah asked.

I shook my head. *"I have no idea. They must live beneath the swamp. They must live and breathe in the goopy water."*

Then the creature turned and looked around.

He sniffed the air like a dog, and I wondered if he could smell us. A chill ran straight down my spine when he looked in our direction, but he didn't see us. He didn't know that we were there.

"We've got to go back and tell Mr. Leonard," I whispered. *"And warn the other campers, too. These things look really dangerous."*

We watched the creature as it roamed around the middle of the swamp. He kept sniffing the air and looking around. He could smell us, I was sure, just like animals can smell humans.

But this was no animal. None that I'd ever heard of, anyway.

This was a Mega-Monster.

Suddenly, the creature looked up at the dark sky and let out a terrible shriek! All three of us jumped. Then the beast sniffed the air again, turned, and looked directly at the thick bushes we were hiding in.

"Don't . . . make . . . a single . . . move," I whispered slowly. The creature seemed to be looking right at us. *"Don't . . . even . . . breathe."*

I heard a clicking sound, and I realized it was my teeth. I bit down hard to make them stop.

The Mega-Monster leaned forward, still looking in our direction. He sniffed the air again, then stood straight up. He looked away.

Whew! He didn't see us.

But just then—disaster.

I didn't know it at the time, but Sandy had been holding back a sneeze. Alas, she couldn't hold it any longer.

"*Ah — CHOOOOO!*" she suddenly burst out. She immediately threw both hands over her mouth.

Now we *were* in trouble.

The huge Mega-Monster spun and looked right at us. He sniffed the air, let out another terrible wail, and began to charge.

He was attacking! We were being attacked by a Mega-Monster!

13

We were in big trouble. The Mega-Monster had spotted us, and he was trudging through the swamp, coming right for us.

"Run!" I shouted, and the three of us sprang from our hiding places and began to run down the trail.

We didn't get far.

There was another Mega-Monster on the trail! This one was even bigger than the one in the swamp, and there was no way we could get around him!

Behind us, the Mega-Monster in the swamp was still charging toward us. On the trail, the other Mega-Monster was blocking our escape!

It was a horrible feeling. While we had been watching the Mega-Monster emerge from the swamp, one had been sneaking up from behind us!

"Through the woods!" I shouted, plunging into the dense shrubbery. "Maybe we can escape through the forest!"

Sandy and Leah followed, and we set off into the woods. I was hoping that since the branches were so thick, we might be able to outrun the giant creatures. Or at least find a place to hide.

"Hurry, Rick!" Leah shouted. I was pushing branches away as fast as I could. Behind us, I heard one of the Mega-Monsters let out a piercing shriek. I hoped we could get away.

Branches snapped and twigs went flying as I plunged deeper and deeper into the forest. I didn't even take the time to look back. I just kept pushing on.

It was working! After a few minutes, we could no longer hear the creatures behind us.

Maybe they couldn't make it through the thick woods. Maybe they were too big.

Whatever the reason, we sure were glad!

After a few more minutes, we stopped to catch our breaths. I don't know if you've ever tried to run through a thick forest before, but let me tell you . . . it's no picnic. All three of us were winded, and we all had scratches on our hands and arms from the tree limbs.

And now we had another problem: how would we get back to camp? Only a half-hour had passed, which meant that we had only ninety minutes of free time left. If we didn't show up for the next activity, maybe everyone would come looking for us.

I looked up into the sky. The clouds were still dark and purple. It hadn't started to rain yet, but it sure looked like a storm was coming.

"We have to try and find our way back," I said.

"Yeah," Leah agreed. "The sooner we get out of the forest, the sooner we can get away from those giant bugs."

"I don't think that they are bugs," I said.

"And let's just be glad they don't have wings."

"Which way do we go?" Sandy asked.

I shook my head. "I'm not sure. We came from that way—" I pointed, "—so maybe if we head over that way." I swung my arm around and pointed in another direction. "Keep your eyes peeled for any more Mega-Monsters."

We started out, and, sure enough, it started to rain. We were soaked to the skin in no time at all. My jeans were wet and soggy, and it was uncomfortable to walk.

But it sure was better than getting gobbled up by one of those monsters.

"I think we're going the wrong way," Sandy said, after we'd walked a little while.

We stopped and looked around. Rain was dripping from the tree branches, and the sky looked as dark as ever.

"Let's go a little bit farther," I said. "If we don't find the camp, we'll stop and wait. Hopefully, someone will come looking for us if we don't make it back."

We started out again, pushing through the thick forest. We had only gone a little ways when

I stopped. Leah and Sandy looked over my shoulder.

"What is it?" Leah asked.

"Look," I said, pointing.

The forest gave way to a lake. Not Willow Lake, that was for sure. This was an entirely different lake. This lake had an island in the middle. Which wasn't a big deal, since lots of lakes in Michigan have islands.

It was what we saw *on* the island that made the three of us stop and stare.

14

It was a castle. An honest-to-goodness castle, like you would see in the movies.

But there was more to it than that.

High above the castle, jagged bolts of lightning pierced through dark storm clouds. Thunder boomed like an earthquake. Rain fell in sheets.

"Where in the world are we?" Leah asked.

"Well, we're somewhere near Rochester Hills, in Michigan, in the United States," I said flatly.

"You're a big help," Leah chided, gently

65

elbowing me. "I mean . . . where is this place? That castle is huge. And there's nothing else around. No cars, no houses. No city. What is going on here?"

"I don't know," I said, shaking my head. I wiped the rain from my face and eyes. "I've never seen anything like this."

"It looks like the lightning is only above the castle," Sandy said, pointing up into the sky. "See?"

She was right! Lightning flashed and cracked, but only above the castle. It was freaky.

"Well, maybe if we can get to the island," Leah suggested, "we can find out where we are. Maybe whoever is there would know how to get back to Camp Willow."

"But how are we going to get there?" I asked. "It's too far to swim."

"Let's walk around," Sandy said. "Maybe we can find something that floats."

We didn't have to go far.

"Look!" Sandy exclaimed. "Over there!"

It was a canoe!

We ran to it. The canoe was upside down,

and there were two paddles beside it.

"This will work!" I said. "Let's turn it over."

We turned the boat over. It was old, and made out of wood.

"Do you think it will float?" Leah asked.

"Only one way to find out," I said. "Let's get it in the water."

We pulled the canoe to the edge of the lake and slid it into the water. We didn't see any leaks.

"I think it'll be okay," I said.

"Who cares?" Sandy said, smiling. "We're soaked already."

The three of us climbed into the boat. I sat in the back, Leah sat in the middle, and Sandy sat in the front. Sandy and I paddled, and the canoe cut through the water with ease.

As we approached the island, lightning and thunder boomed high in the sky. The rain came down in buckets, and soon, Leah was cupping her hands to bail out the water that had collected in the boat.

We were halfway to the island when Sandy suddenly screamed.

"What?!?!?" I shouted. *"What is it?!?!?"*

"It's . . . it's one of them!" she shrieked, pointing with her canoe paddle.

I looked at what she was pointing at, and froze.

A Mega-Monster!

He was in the water, looking right at us, and he was only a few feet away!

"Paddle!" Leah screamed. *"That thing is going to get us!"*

I paddled like I had never paddled before. Water churned and splashed. I turned us away from the Mega-Monster in the water and we all began to paddle as hard as we could.

The Mega-Monster was really fast in the water. We were a little faster, but not by much.

"Keep going!" I shouted frantically. "He's right behind us! We've got to stay ahead of him!"

It seemed to take us forever to reach the shore.

The monster was still behind us, and as soon as we hit land we jumped out of the canoe and began running to the castle.

"Oh no!" Sandy shouted, pointing. "Look up ahead!"

It was a wall. A tall, stone wall went all the way around the castle.

There was no way to get in!

"We'll have to climb!" I shouted. "There's no time to do anything else!"

Behind us, the Mega-Monster had just reached the shore. His eyes were focused on us, and he didn't look happy.

He looked *hungry*.

We continued running until we reached the wall that surrounded the castle. Above us, lightning continued to blast and crash in the dark sky.

"*Climb!*" I screamed. I leapt up and grasped the brick wall, and immediately slid back down. The rocks were slippery, and I couldn't get a grip to pull myself up. I jumped up and tried again, but the same thing happened. My fingers slipped, and I fell to the ground.

And behind us, the giant Mega-Monster was racing toward us, snarling and growling, arms outstretched. His sharp claws were curling in and out, in and out, and I knew that it would only be seconds before he was upon us.

All of a sudden, Sandy spread out her hands. Rain streaked down her face.

"Quick!" she said. *"Grab my hand!"*

"What?!?!?" I shouted.

"I'll explain later!" she said. *"Just grab my hands! It's the only way!"*

I had no idea what she was talking about, but I took her hand in mine, and Leah took her other hand. Behind us, the Mega-Monster was still charging like mad. He would be upon us in seconds.

"Hang on tight!" Sandy ordered.

And what happened next was unbelievable.

16

Sandy began to fly!

It's crazy, I know. You don't have to tell me! But that's exactly what happened. Sandy's feet left the ground, and I could feel her hand pulling mine. She began to rise up into the air!

All the while, the Mega-Monster was getting closer and closer.

Sandy was rising higher still, and I held her hand tightly in mine. My feet suddenly left the ground, and the ground below me fell away. I was being lifted up in the air!

And it was a good thing, too! Because the Mega-Monster reached out his claws and almost got me! He was right below us! When he found out that he couldn't grab us, he started to climb the wall, but it was too slippery. He slid back to the ground.

Meanwhile, we were floating in the air just above the top of the stone wall. Then we moved sideways and began to descend safely on the other side of the wall.

When my feet touched the ground, I looked at Sandy in amazement.

"Don't worry," she said. "I'm not a freak or anything. I'll explain later." She looked at Leah, and then they both looked at me. Leah looked like she was about to say something, but she didn't speak.

"What?" I asked Leah. "Is there something I should know?"

Leah and Sandy looked at each other again.

"Later," Leah said. "I'll tell you later."

"Are you going to tell me that you can fly, too?" I asked.

"No," she said, shaking her head. "I can't fly.

But . . . well . . . I'll tell you later."

I dropped the issue. If Leah had something to tell me, she would tell me when she was ready. Right now, I was still freaked out by the fact that Sandy could fly!

"Come on," Sandy said. "Let's go see if anyone is in the castle."

Here, on the other side of the stone wall, the sky was as dark as ever. The rain continued to pour, and lightning streaked across the sky.

We ran across wet grass toward the castle. Water squished and splashed beneath our feet.

"There's a door over there!" I said, pointing as I ran. Every few seconds I turned around to make sure that we weren't being chased by any Mega-Monsters.

We were almost to the door when I heard something in the sky above me. I looked up, stopped running, and shouted.

"LEAH! SANDY! Look out!"

Leah and Sandy stopped, turned, and looked up. They both screamed.

Above us, swooping and diving, were bats. Dozens of them.

But these weren't ordinary bats. They were huge! These bats were the size of eagles — *and they were attacking!*

17

I dove to the wet ground just as a giant bat swooped down to snag me in his claws, but he missed. He squeaked and squealed angrily as he spun off, but I knew I wasn't safe yet.

Leah and Sandy had also dived to the ground, and they were rolling toward the castle. I started doing the same. The grass was so wet, it was like rolling in a stream.

But it was working! I could hear the bats swarming above us, but they couldn't grab us.

Rolling, rolling, rolling. In front of me, Sandy

had reached the castle. She jumped to her feet and sprang to the castle. I could see her standing by the huge door.

"Hurry!" she screamed.

Leah was next, and she leapt from the ground and bounded up to Sandy.

Now it was my turn. I stopped, jumped up, and sprinted.

Suddenly, I was snagged from behind! Something had caught my shirt. I struggled to get away, but whatever was holding me was really strong. I could hear the heavy flapping of wings, and I knew right away that it was a bat.

Sandy and Leah were screaming at me. I was trying to struggle away from the flying beast, waving my arms and spinning around.

The creature was strong. I could feel him pulling at me, and I could feel myself being lifted off the ground.

Leah and Sandy raced to my rescue. Leah grabbed my shirt, and Sandy started swinging her arms at the bat.

"Fall to the ground!" Leah shouted.

I dove to the grass and while Leah and Sandy

swung their arms at the enormous bat.

Finally, the bat gave up. He let go of my shirt and flew off. Thankfully, the other bats were flying off, too. I could see them flying back up into the dark sky, disappearing into the clouds. Maybe they decided that we were too big to be a meal for them.

We ran for the castle door. I pounded it with my fist—and got a surprise.

The door was open!

It hadn't been closed all the way, and when I hit it with my hand, it swung open a little bit. There was a dim light coming from inside, but I couldn't see anything through the crack.

"Hello?" I called out. "Anybody home?"

No answer.

"Hello?" I called out again.

Still no answer. I pushed the door open a few inches. Inside, I could see a flaming torch on the wall. Stone glistened in the pale light.

"Anybody home?" I called out, louder this time. Still, there was no answer.

"Rick," Sandy said quietly. "Stop."

I turned to her. "Huh?" I asked. But she

wasn't looking at me. Sandy and Leah both were looking out toward the big stone wall. I turned to see what they were looking at — and I froze in terror.

18

Eyes. Hundreds of gleaming, yellow eyes were glaring at us.

"What are they?" Leah asked quietly.

"I don't know," I replied.

"Me neither," Sandy answered.

The eyes were near the stone wall, but we couldn't see what kind of animals they were. It was too dark, and it was still raining too hard.

But one thing was for sure: whatever kind of creatures they were, they were coming closer.

"Come on," I said. I pushed the castle door

open.

Sandy asked."Are you sure this is a good idea?"

"We don't have much of a choice," I replied. "I'm not hanging out to see what those things want."

Without another word, I slipped through the door and into the castle. Leah and Sandy followed, and I closed the door behind us.

We were in what appeared to be a long hallway. Torches were lit on the walls, and the ceiling was very high.

And *noises*. We could hear noises coming from a long ways away.

"Let's go," I said, starting off in the direction of the sounds. "Someone is here. Maybe they can help us."

We set out down the hall. Outside, we could hear thunder booming and crashing.

The sounds grew louder. It sounded like voices talking. There were other noises, too. Sounds of clinking glass and shuffling. As we continued walking, the sounds grew louder.

Finally, after what seemed like a long time, we

came to a closed, wood door. A thin strip of light glowed at the bottom of it. We could hear talking and loud noises coming from the other side.

I looked at Leah and Sandy, and they looked at me. Leah reached out her hand and knocked.

Suddenly, the talking stopped. The shuffling ceased.

Then: *footsteps.* Footsteps grew louder, coming closer and closer to the door. The doorknob jiggled, and the heavy wood door swung open.

And we gasped.

19

I guess it was just the surprise of seeing the man that caused us to gasp. Because not only was it a man, but it was a man that we knew.

It was the camp director, Mr. Williams!

We freaked, and so did he. Mr. Williams was the last person I expected to see! He was wearing a white lab coat, and in one hand he held a glass beaker.

"Children!" he boomed. He looked shocked to see us. "What are you doing here?!?!?!"

"Well, uh, ummmm . . . ." I stammered.

"Never mind us," Sandy said. "What are *you* doing here?"

"I live here," he explained. "But how did you —"

"We went to the swamp to find the Mega-Monsters. We got lost in the forest, and we found this place."

Mr. Williams's eyes just about popped out of his head. I was sure that they were going to fall on the floor and break like glass marbles.

"You're very lucky," he said. "The Mega-Monsters are the most dangerous creatures I've created."

"*Created?!?!?!*" I said. "*You made them?!?!?*" It sounded incredible.

"Yes, I made them . . . sort of. Now I'm trying to find a way to get rid of them."

It seemed unbelievable. At the camp, Mr. Williams seemed so . . . so geeky. Here, in the castle, he looked more like some sort of mad scientist.

"What about the bats?" Leah asked. "Did you create them, too?"

"No. The bats are real bats. But they used to

be very small. Not much bigger than a mouse, really. I fed them my experimental potion and it backfired. I was trying to make them smaller, but it didn't work."

"And the eyes that we saw? In the darkness near the wall?"

"Crickets," Mr. Williams explained. "Another one of my experiments. The crickets have grown to the size of large dogs."

Crickets the size of dogs?!?! That's crazy!

"But how can—"

Mr. Williams raised his hands, and I stopped speaking. "Please," he said. "I've kept this a secret for a long time. But now that you're here, you might as well know the truth. Come into my laboratory and I will explain everything."

If I thought things had been freaky already, it was nothing compared to what Mr. Williams was about to tell us.

20

Mr. Williams's laboratory was cluttered with shelves and tables, all filled with jars and test tubes and beakers. On one table, beakers filled with colorful liquids fizzed and bubbled.

We all sat down at a table, and Mr. Williams began to speak.

"I've always wanted to be a scientist," he said, "but every experiment I try seems to get screwed up. The Mega-Monsters aren't really monsters at all . . . they are harmless crayfish. Or . . . *were* . . . harmless crayfish."

"What?!?!?" Sandy exclaimed, her eyes wide.

Mr. Williams nodded. "It's true," he said. "I accidentally spilled one of my experimental potions into the lake one day. All of the crayfish began to grow and change. They became horrible, horrible creatures. They became the creatures now known as the Mega-Monsters. They grew to enormous size, and their bodies changed into hideous swamp creatures."

"You . . . you mean that . . . that those *things* are actually *crayfish?!?!*" I asked.

Mr. Williams nodded his head. "Yes," he said. "They are only crayfish. It was my potion that changed them into the awful beasts that you now see."

"But how do you change them back?" Leah asked. "Does the potion wear off over time?"

"I'm afraid that it won't wear off," Mr. Williams answered. "I've been searching for years to try and find a potion that would change them back into crayfish. So far, I've only succeeded in creating giant bats and crickets. However, I do have a new experimental potion that might work . . . but it might already be too late."

"But how do *you* get here?" I asked. "If the Mega-Monsters are so dangerous, how do you get back to the camp?"

"I have a small helicopter that I use. I can fly from my castle to a small field that isn't far from the camp. No one knows about the helicopter, and until now, no one knew that I had anything to do with the Mega-Monsters."

"And what about the weather?" Leah asked. "How come there's so much thunder and lightning around your castle?"

Mr. Williams looked proud. "Ah, yes," he said. "My only experiment that has ever worked. Come. I will show you."

He stood up, and we followed him through another door and into a dim hallway. Our feet swished on the stone floor. Soon, we came to a series of steps, and we climbed up. The staircase wound up, higher and higher, and we came to another door. Mr. Williams pulled out some keys from his pocket, unlocked the door, and stepped inside. We followed.

The small area we were in looked like a

control room. There were windows all around, and we could look out and see for miles. I could see the water below, and the shore on the other side of the lake.

But all around us, above the castle, lightning flashed. Thunder boomed wildly. The wind and rain blew like mad.

"My finest invention," Mr. Williams beamed. "From here, I can control the weather around my castle."

"You can do what?!?!" I asked. Controlling the weather seemed unbelievable.

"Yes, it's true," he explained. "I can control the weather, but only around my castle and the lake. Watch."

Mr. Williams reached out and grasped a lever. There was a button on it, and he pressed it. Instantly, a flash of lightning lit up the sky, followed closely by a tremendous boom!

"That's cool!" Sandy and I said at the same time.

"Yes, it's a lot of fun. With these here—" He pointed to another row of levers. "—I can control the wind and the rain. Even the clouds. Right now, I have all of the controls set at 'severe thunderstorm' to keep most people away. Most people—"

Mr. Williams was interrupted by a siren, and a blinking red light. He reached out, flipped several buttons, and a television screen jumped to life.

"Oh no!" Mr. Williams exclaimed, staring at the images on the television screen. "The Mega-Monsters! They've made it over the rock wall! They've destroyed my helicopter!"

It was true. As we watched the screen, we could see the Mega-Monsters tearing apart the helicopter.

"They know that you're inside the castle," Mr. Williams explained, "and they are going to make sure that you don't leave."

"What?!?!??" Leah exclaimed. "What do you mean?!?!"

"The Mega-Monsters know that you're here," he repeated. "They are furious. They know that you're here, and they will do everything they can to keep you from leaving."

"What will happen if they capture us?" Sandy

asked. "What will they do?"

I looked at the TV monitor and saw one of the Mega-Monsters pick up a piece of the broken helicopter. He opened up his mouth and bit into it, chewing up the metal like it was candy.

Things were *not* looking very good.

21

We were trapped. Mr. Williams's helicopter was completely demolished, and, as we watched the television monitor, more and more Mega-Monsters were climbing over the rock wall. They were climbing over one another to make it over the top of the stone wall.

"What are we going to do?" Sandy asked. "How are we going to get out of here?"

Then I suddenly remembered something. *Sandy had been able to fly!* I didn't know how . . . but maybe she could use her power to help us escape.

"Sandy!" I exclaimed. "You can—"

Sandy suddenly shot me a nasty glance, and I could tell she didn't want me to keep talking.

"What?" Mr. Williams asked. "What can she do?"

"Oh, nothing," I said. "Are you sure there isn't any other way out of here?"

Mr. Williams paused and gave a thoughtful look.

"Well," he began, "there is. There is another way out, but it would be dangerous."

"What is it?" Leah asked. "Do you have a boat or something?"

"No. It would be too dangerous to use a boat now. Perhaps—"

He stopped speaking, and stroked his chin as he looked out the window. "Yes," he continued. "Perhaps that just might work."

"What?" I pleaded. "What might work?"

"There is an underground tunnel," Mr. Williams explained. "It runs beneath the castle and under the lake to the other side. It comes out in a clump of trees. There is an iron door there to keep the Mega-Monsters out. The only problem is that the creatures know where the door is. They would be watching for us. But—"

He stopped again, thinking. He was silent for a long time. It was driving me nuts.

"But what?" I asked. If there was a chance we could make it off the island safely, I wanted to know about it.

"Yes, there is a chance," Mr. Williams said. "But I'll need your help. All of you. There is a chance we can escape safely. But you'll have to do exactly what I say."

"Anything," Leah said. "We'll do anything to get out of this place."

But when Mr. Williams explained what we would have to do, I about fell right out of my chair.

22

"What we need to do," Mr. Williams explained, "is get the Mega-Monsters to eat my new experimental potion. I think I've finally perfected it, and it should change the creatures back into small crayfish."

"How are we going to do that?" I asked.

"Simple. The Mega-Monsters eat fish, just like crayfish. I've taken hundreds of tiny sardines and soaked them in my new potion. We need to get the Mega-Monsters to eat the sardines. Then, they'll shrink back to crayfish."

"But how do we get them to eat the sardines?" Leah asked. "It's too dangerous to go outside."

"We will take the tunnel under the lake to the other side. When the Mega-Monsters around the castle see what's going on, they'll swim to where we are on the other side of the lake. We'll throw the sardines out near the shore, then get back into the tunnel. Hopefully, the Mega-Monsters will pick up their scent. They will eat them, and all of the hideous creatures will become crayfish again."

It sounded like it might work! At least, Mr. Williams seemed excited about it.

"Quickly!" he exclaimed. "Let's go back to the lab. You three can help me load up the sardines in a wheelbarrow."

When we reached the lab, Mr. Williams sprang into action. He brought in a big, old wheelbarrow, and set it by a refrigerator. Inside the fridge were dozens and dozens of jars filled with sardines. They looked like little gray fish all packed together.

"Help me load these into the wheelbarrow," Mr. Williams ordered.

The three of us sprang into action. In no time

at all we had carefully filled the wheelbarrow with jars of sardines.

"Are you sure this is going to work?" Leah asked. I, myself, had doubts.

"Yes," Mr. Williams assured us. "The Mega-Monsters will see us, but they'll smell the sardines. They love fish, especially sardines."

"But what if they don't change back into crayfish?" Sandy asked. "Then what?"

"Oh, they'll turn back into crayfish, I promise you," Mr. Williams said. "I know that for a fact. I just hope that it changes them back to crayfish fast."

Mr. Williams lifted the wheelbarrow and led us through a narrow passageway. It got really dark. When we came to a door, he stopped, set the wheelbarrow down, and pulled out his keys. The door opened, exposing a dark, tube-like tunnel made of stone.

"This has been here since the castle was built hundreds of years ago," Mr. Williams explained.

"Are you sure it's safe?" I asked.

"It's fine," Mr. Williams said. "It's just dark." He reached into his pocket and pulled out a small candle, struck a match, and lit the wick. The tiny flame flickered and swayed, and shadows danced about. He handed the candle to Sandy.

"You carry the candle," he told her, "and I'll push the wheelbarrow."

We were off. We would travel through the tunnel, open up the jars of sardines, and toss them over the ground for the Mega-Monsters to eat. If we were lucky, the plan would work, and we would be able to return to camp without having to worry about the horrible creatures.

Unfortunately, that's not what was going to happen.

Our luck was about to run out.

23

The tunnel was long. It seemed so weird to be walking through it, like walking through a long worm that stretched out beneath the lake. The air felt sticky and damp, and our footsteps echoed in the dim light.

Suddenly, the tunnel stopped at what appeared to be an iron wall.

"Here we are," Mr. Williams said. He lowered the wheelbarrow and again dug in his pocket for his keys. "We'll have to be careful," he said. "I'll go out first, to make sure there are no Mega-

Monsters around."

The door was round, and Mr. Williams inserted the key and turned the lock. There was a *clunking* sound, and the door slowly chugged open. He poked his head out.

"All clear," he said. "Come on."

Sandy set her candle down, and Leah and I followed her as she stepped out into the rain. Across the lake, the clouds boiled above the castle. We could see Mega-Monsters all over the place. We could even hear them shrieking and howling. Thankfully, we were hidden in the thick brush, and the creatures couldn't see us.

Mr. Williams pushed the wheelbarrow out of the tunnel.

"Just unscrew the jars and pour the sardines all over the ground," he ordered. "The Mega-Monsters will smell them."

We did as he asked. Man . . . those sardines really smelled! It was awful.

Just as we were emptying the last of the jars, Leah shouted.

"Over there!"

We turned. A Mega-Monster—a *huge*

one—was climbing out of the water. He had spotted us!

"Come on!" Mr. Williams shouted. "Back to the tunnel!"

We climbed back into the tunnel just as the Mega-Monster got out of the water. Mr. Williams closed the round, iron door. Sandy picked up the candle.

"Let's go!" Mr. Williams said. We started running through the tunnel, and our pounding feet echoed down the dark, damp corridor. We could go a lot faster now that we'd left the wheelbarrow behind, and we made it back to the castle in no time.

"Up to the control room!" Mr. Williams ordered. "We can see what's going on from there!"

We bounded down halls, around corners, up winding stairs. Our footsteps echoed as we ran.

Finally, we made it to the control tower. Leah, Sandy, and I followed Mr. Williams inside. We looked out the windows.

"Oh no!" Mr. Williams shouted. "Oh no! It can't be! Oh no!"

I looked across the lake—and I couldn't believe what I was seeing.

24

The Mega-Monsters had turned back into crayfish — sort of. Only they hadn't gotten smaller — they'd grown *larger!*

Oh no!

The Mega-Monsters that had eaten the sardines had grown to the size of houses! What's more, they had changed. They each had two large claws — one on each arm — and they'd grown an extra pair of arms as well! They were the most awful, ugly creatures I had ever seen.

"Oh my gosh!" Sandy exclaimed. "They're

gargantuan!"

The monsters had eaten all of the sardines, and now they were returning to the water.

"It's impossible!" Mr. Williams gasped.

"What do we do now?" I asked.

"We must stop them! With those claws, they will be able to tear their way into the castle!"

"But how?" Leah asked. "How are we going to stop them now?"

"I think I know what I did wrong. I think I can make another potion that will change them."

"That's what you said last time," I said.

"Yes, but . . . well, I don't have time to explain. Here's what we'll do:

"You three stay here and control the weather. Make the conditions as bad as you can." He pounded the air with his fists. "Use the lightning control to blast away at the creatures. Make it rain hard so they can't see. And the wind!" He waved his arms back and forth. "Make the wind blow very hard so it is a struggle for them. I'll go to my laboratory and mix up another batch of potion. I know what went wrong. I can fix it."

I sure hoped he was right. If he wasn't, we

would all be goners.

Leah, Sandy and I took our seats in front of the equipment. There were a lot of blinking lights and flashing dials, like the cockpit of an airplane. Leah would control the wind, Sandy would control the rain, and I would control the lightning.

"Don't let them get near the castle," Mr. Williams ordered. "Try and keep them as far away as possible. I've got to go to my laboratory."

I grasped the lightning lever in my hand. It felt very powerful. Leah and Sandy grabbed their levers, and Mr. Williams disappeared through the door.

"If I wasn't so scared, this might be kind of cool," Leah said.

I looked at Sandy. I had been dying to ask her how she was able to fly when she pulled Leah and me over the wall.

"Sandy," I began, "how did you do that? How did you fly up in the air like you did?"

She looked at me, and then looked away, like she didn't want to talk about it.

"It's okay if you don't want to answer," I said.

"But I really do want to know. That was really freaky."

Sandy reached into her pocket and pulled out a stone. She handed it to me. It was a little bit bigger than a quarter, and it had a dragonfly carved into it.

"Last summer when my family visited Mackinac Island, my brother and I had some weird things happen to us. I can't explain it all now, but this rock enables me to fly. Not for long, because it's not very powerful. The power wears out quickly. But it allows me to fly short distances, as long as I have it with me."

"Wow," I whispered, rolling the stone through my hands. I wished that I had a stone like that.

I looked at Leah. "And what about you? Can you fly, too?"

Leah looked at Sandy, and they both looked at me. Leah spoke.

"I was going to wait to tell you this. No, I can't fly, but I can—"

"Look out!" Sandy suddenly shrieked. She had glanced out the window. Whatever Leah was going to tell me would have to wait.

A Mega-Monster, with claws and everything, was climbing over the stone wall!

"Rick! Stop him!" Leah shouted.

I grasped the lightning lever tightly. I had no idea how to aim or anything. I just grabbed the lever and pushed the button.

"Here goes nothing," I whispered.

25

A blast of white lightning shot through the sky like a rocket. The bolt hit the wall with a thundering explosion, sending the creature reeling back. Giant claws spun in the air as the ugly creature retreated.

"Great job!" Sandy exclaimed.

More creatures were approaching. They were the weirdest-looking things I had ever seen in my life. The Mega-Monsters had morphed into half-crayfish, half-ape beasts. Never in my worst nightmares had I ever imagined such a horrifying creature.

"Let's get 'em," I said, and we began giving the monsters everything we could. Sandy blasted them with rain, and Leah gave them powerful, heaving winds. I let lightning bolts fly in every direction, and the sharp blades seared the clouds.

"Hey! This is kind of cool!" Leah exclaimed. "I kind of like having control of the weather!"

"Me too," I agreed. "I wish I had one of these contraptions at home."

The strange creatures kept coming, and we spent the next few minutes battering the beasts with the elements. The lightning worked the best, because when I blasted one of the monsters, it sent the creature flying. The bolt didn't kill it, but it sure slowed the monster down.

"Great shot!" Leah said, raising her hand up in the air. I slapped her palm, exchanging a high-five.

We quickly learned how to use the switches and levers. Sandy made it rain so hard that it was hard to see the stone wall that surrounded the castle. Leah, in control of the wind, created gusts so strong that it blew the rain sideways.

And I was almost having fun with the lightning. I was sending bolts every which way, and they tore through the rain and wind like jagged knives.

The Mega-Monsters came. The ones that had eaten the sardines were gruesome. They were even uglier than they had been. One of them looked like he could have been half-monster, half-crayfish . . . but he was as big as a house!

"Get him, Rick!" Sandy exclaimed.

I twisted the lever and pressed a button on the panel.

A searing bolt of lightning suddenly shot from the sky. It hit the water right in front of the charging Mega-Monster! The creature drew back, then disappeared beneath the churning, dark water.

We all cheered. We were going to be able to hold them off, after all.

"We're going to do it!" I shouted.

But I had spoke too soon. The minute I finished my sentence, the windows all around us exploded! Sharp glass flew everywhere, and the wind and rain poured into the control room.

We all ducked, covering our heads to protect us from the razor-sharp glass that flew all around us.

"What happened??!?" Sandy screamed above the howling wind and rain.

But there was no need to answer her. A gruesome arm suddenly appeared through the window. And a face.

It was a Mega-Monster! One of the ones that hadn't eaten the sardines! He must have come up from behind and climbed up onto the roof!

And in the next horrifying moment, he leapt into the control room.

I screamed. Sandy screamed. Leah screamed. The Mega-Monster was only a few feet away.

This was it. There would be no escape, this time.

We were goners.

26

With a powerful sweep of his arm, the Mega-Monster smashed a table. The wood splintered, and pieces crumbled to the floor. The beast let out a yell that would straighten out a new hairdo.

We tried to run to the door, but the creature jumped ahead and blocked our escape. He swung his arm at me, but I ducked out of the way, falling to the floor and rolling to the other side of the control room.

Leah and Sandy were cornered.

The beast attacked.

Suddenly, I saw Sandy pop up from beneath the beast! Then Leah! They had dropped to the floor and ran between the Mega-Monster's legs!

Just then, I had an idea.

"Get away from him!" I shouted, waving to Leah and Sandy. "Get as far away as you can!"

They ran toward me, and I grasped the lever that controlled the lightning. I aimed for only a split-second, then pressed the button.

Instantly, an enormous bright flash and a tremendous explosion rocked the control tower! We were thrown to the ground, and debris fell all around us. Wind and rain continued to pour in as the control room around us exploded!

"What happened?!?!?" Sandy shouted.

"I aimed a lightning bolt at the control tower!" I shouted back. "Look out!"

A piece of the control room, part of the wall, fell in. Sandy rolled sideways, getting out of the way the instant before the wall smashed to the ground.

"Are you nuts?!?!?" Leah exclaimed. "You could have wiped us out!"

"Did you want to be a snack-cake for the

Mega-Monster?" I replied.

We climbed to our feet, brushing away the pieces of the tower that had fallen upon us. I had a small glass cut on my hand, but it wasn't bad. Actually, considering what had just happened, we were all pretty lucky.

"The Mega-Monster!" Sandy exclaimed. "He's gone!"

We looked around. The control room was charred and black. Parts of it were on fire.

But there was no sign of the Mega-Monster. At least, not on or around the control tower.

But in the lake, all around the island, was a different story.

There were Mega-Monsters of all sizes. The ones that had eaten the sardines were huge, and had enormous claws. The monsters that hadn't eaten the fish were just as ugly, like the one that had attacked the control tower.

But now, there was nothing we could do. The lightning blast had destroyed the control tower. We were powerless to use the wind, rain, or lightning to stop the attacking Mega-Monsters. Soon, they would reach the island and climb over the stone wall. Then they would attack the castle.

Suddenly, Mr. Williams appeared. The door was gone, of course. There was only an open stairway.

"What happened?!??!" he asked.

"We were attacked," I explained. "The control tower was destroyed by a bolt of lightning. We didn't have any other choice."

I thought that he was going to be really mad, but he didn't say anything about the damage. His eyes grew wide, and his face was lit up with excitement.

"I have it!"he exclaimed. "I have a potion that will work! I've already tested it, so I know that it'll work!"

"It might already be too late!" I shouted. "Look!"

The Mega-Monsters had succeeded in tearing down part of the stone wall. Now they were pouring into the castle grounds!

"We've got to escape now!" Mr. Williams said.

"But how?" I asked. "We have to make sure they eat your new batch of potion!"

"There isn't any more time! The monsters will

be able to tear apart the castle! I've already soaked a few cases of sardines in my new potion. We'll have to escape through the tunnel while we still can! We can only hope that the creatures find the sardines in the laboratory, and eat them!"

Outside, the terrible creatures were attacking. We had held them off for as long as we could, but now they had reached the castle. We could hear their awful shrieks and howls.

"Let's go!" Mr. Williams ordered. "We have to escape through the tunnel! It's our only hope!"

We burst out of the control tower and followed Mr. Williams down the spiraling stone stairs.

"Faster!" he urged. "They'll be able to smash their way through the castle in no time at all!"

We sprang down a long hallway and around sharp corners. But when we came to the tunnel, our hopes vanished.

The tunnel was filled with water!

Leah gasped. Sandy gasped. I gasped.

Water was pouring into the castle through the tunnel. Mr. Williams stopped, and placed both hands on his head in frustration.

"The creatures have crushed the tunnel!" Mr. Williams exclaimed. He raised one hand to his head, and closed his eyes. Outside, I could hear the monsters smashing at the stone castle. It wouldn't be long before they crushed the walls and came inside.

"We're doomed now," Mr. Williams continued, sadly shaking his head. "There is no way out."

Things weren't looking very good.

27

Outside the castle, we could hear the terrible creatures pounding at the castle wall. Rocks were crumbling, and the beasts were screeching and wailing. I couldn't bear to even *think* about being snared by one of their huge, powerful claws.

"Let's go back to the control tower," Mr. Williams commanded. "From there, we can at least see all the way around the castle. We can find the best possible escape route. The only thing we'll be able to do now is make a run for it."

I didn't know how we would be able to make

a 'run for it' when we were on an island, but one thing was for sure: I wanted to stay as far away from those creatures as I possibly could.

Back through the castle we ran, through winding halls and up stone steps. All the while, we could hear the sounds of the Mega-Monsters battering away outside the castle. It sounded like there were hundreds of the beasts, scraping and clawing at the stone.

We reached the control tower. The fires had gone out, and the room was a wet mess of destroyed debris.

The castle grounds below us were filled with the monsters. There were so many of them, they were climbing all over one another. Mr. Williams spoke.

"This is all my fault," Mr. Williams said. "I created these awful beasts, and now, there's no stopping them."

A chill ran down my spine. If Mr. Williams had given up hope, things must be pretty bad.

Suddenly, I had an idea! My eyes grew wide, and I almost shouted.

"The canoe!" I exclaimed. "The one we used

to get here! Maybe we can use it to leave the island!"

"I'm afraid it wouldn't be possible," Mr. Williams said.

"It might be!" Leah said. "If we can make it to the canoe before the creatures spot us! Look!" She pointed down at the Mega-Monsters still attacking the castle. The creatures hadn't succeeded in getting inside yet, but they were close.

"Most of the monsters are up here, near the castle," Leah continued. "There aren't any by the water. If we can make it to the water, maybe we can paddle fast enough to get away from them!"

Mr. Williams thought for a moment. He scratched his head.

"You know," he said, "that just might work. There is a back door that emerges on the other side of the stone wall. Most of the Mega-Monsters are up here, in the front."

"That's it, then!" I said. "We've got to try!"

"Yes!" Sandy exclaimed. "It's worth a shot!"

"Come!" Mr. Williams ordered. "Down the hall and around the back of my laboratory!"

We followed Mr. Williams as he dashed down the hall. Our footsteps drummed the cold stone beneath our feet, and the sounds echoed down the hall. Sandy was running beside me.

"Sandy," I whispered as I ran. *"Can't you do what you did when we needed to get over the stone wall? Can't you hold our hands and fly?"*

"No," she whispered back as we both ran around a corner. Mr. Williams and Leah were in front of us. *"I wish I could, but I don't think the tiny stone is that powerful. I don't think that the four of us would even get off the ground."*

Rats. It would be cool to fly again!

"Here we are!" Mr. Williams shouted. We stopped at a large, wood door. Once again, Mr. Williams pulled out his keys, inserted one into the lock, and turned the knob.

"Stay here," he said. "I'll go check it out." He opened the door and peered outside. Then he stepped outside and closed the door behind him.

"Now what?" Leah asked.

"We wait," I replied. "Let's just wait until Mr. Williams returns."

The seconds seemed like hours. Finally, the

door opened. Mr. Williams appeared, waving us outside.

"They're all on the other side of the castle!" he exclaimed. "Now's our chance! We'll run to the canoe. Rick, you grab the front of it, and I'll grab the back. We'll slide it into the water as fast as we can. Leah and Sandy . . . you two run right behind us and jump into the canoe the moment it hits the water. Everybody got it?"

We all nodded.

"Okay . . . on the count of three, we'll start running. Don't look back. Just keep running until we reach the canoe. One . . . two—"

I took a breath.

"Three!"

Ready or not, we were on our way to the canoe, in our last effort to leave the island and get away from the terrible Mega-Monsters.

But there was one terrible problem with our plan: we had forgotten about the giant bats.

127

I ran like I had never ran before, pumping my legs as hard as I could. Behind me, I heard a thundering crash. I turned to see the giant monsters knocking over a castle wall. They had succeeded in tearing it down, and now they were entering the castle!

It was what we needed. The Mega-Monsters were focusing their attention on the castle, and there weren't any looking our way.

I turned back around and caught sight of the canoe on the shore.

Almost there.

Maybe we'll make it, after all, I thought. *Maybe this plan will work. If we can paddle fast enough, maybe we can out-distance the creatures! And maybe if the creatures got into Mr. Williams's laboratory, they would eat the sardines soaked in potion. Then, maybe they would shrink back to normal-sized crayfish.*

The only thing I could do was hope.

Then:

A shriek from above. It was a high-pitched squeal, and it didn't sound like it came from one of the Mega-Monsters. The Mega-Monster's screams were throaty and gruff, and this new sound was more like a whining screech.

Like . . . .

Oh no!

The claws ripped the back of my shirt open just as I realized what was happening.

Bats! The giant bats were attacking!

I fell to the ground and rolled. The bat that had attacked me hadn't hurt me, but he'd sure torn up my shirt!

"The bats!" Mr. Williams cried. "I forgot about them!"

The flying beasts were all around us, swooping and diving like deranged eagles.

"Keep rolling on the ground!" Mr. Williams shouted. "They can't get you if you keep rolling on the ground! If we can keep rolling, they'll leave us alone!"

Man . . . this just wasn't my day. If we would have stayed at the camp, we'd be doing something fun right now . . . like fishing or hiking or boating.

Now, we had to worry about not only the Mega-Monsters, but giant bats!

I kept rolling and rolling, and every second or two I caught a glimpse of the others doing the same.

And bats. There were dozens of them, swooping up and down, diving and darting.

But so far, they hadn't been able to snag us. By rolling on the ground, we were moving too much for them to sink their teeth and claws into us.

Wham! I hit something so hard that I winced in pain. I had struck something solid, and it had stopped me from rolling.

A tree. I had hit a tree!

I spun on the ground and began to roll away, toward the lake . . . but it was too late. I heard a loud squeal from close by, and felt the heavy tug at my shirt.

Suddenly, I was lifted off the ground! A bat had caught me!

29

The ground fell away as the awful creature carried me up into the air. Below me, I could hear Leah and Sandy screaming.

I began swinging my arms like mad, trying to hit the creature. It was no use.

Then, as the creature spun around the tree, heading higher and higher into the sky, my arm hit something. I reacted quickly and swung my hand . . . and grabbed a tree branch.

The bat screeched. I could hear his wings beating the air as he tried to pull me away.

But I wasn't going to let him.

I reached out with my other arm and grabbed the branch, holding on to save my life. I couldn't let the bat carry me off!

The tree branch trembled as I held it, my arms wrapped tightly about it. Other bats were swarming up in the air, and I hoped that they didn't try to help their buddy carry me away. I might be able to get away from one bat—but two or three?

Never.

Suddenly, there was a loud tearing sound. My shirt had ripped completely in half, and the bat was holding the torn part.

I was free!

I began climbing down the branch, sinking within the protection of the limbs. The other bats had joined in, and they were all swarming around the tree like a bunch of angry hornets.

But the branches were too thick for them to get at me!

They screeched and squealed angrily as they spun faster and faster around the tree. I kept climbing, and didn't stop until I had reached the trunk.

I looked up.

The bats had given up, and were now swirling off, high up into the clouds.

"Rick!" Sandy shouted from below. "You saved us!"

"Yeah!" chimed Leah. "You distracted all of them away from us!"

I climbed down the tree, hung on the last branch, and dropped to the ground.

"Good work," Mr. Williams said. "That was quick thinking."

"I think it was more luck than anything," I replied.

"Come on," Leah said. "We have to make it to the water!"

The four of us took off running again.

Finally, we reached the canoe. I did exactly what Mr. Williams had told me to do: I grabbed the front of the canoe, and began pulling it into the water. Mr. Williams grabbed the back of the canoe, and we heaved it into the lake. Leah and Sandy jumped in with so much force that the canoe almost tipped over!

I jumped in the front of the boat, followed by Mr. Williams.

"Paddle, Rick! Paddle!" he urged. I grabbed the paddle and thrust the blade into the water. The canoe began slicing through the water. I began to think that we were going to make it—until I heard a loud screech coming from the island.

We all turned to see a huge creature near the castle. There were several others around, but this particular creature was looking right at us. He seemed to be pointing one of his huge claws right at us! We'd been spotted!

Then the other Mega-Monsters saw us! They abandoned the castle and began heading toward the water.

If we were going to make it, we were going to have to paddle like mad.

"Come on Rick!" Leah urged. "Paddle faster!"

The thought of being a snack for one of those nasty creatures made me cringe. Mom and Dad would be furious.

But then again, if I wound up being a snack for a Mega-Monster, Mom and Dad couldn't really be mad. At least not at me!

Water churned and splashed as Mr. Williams and I paddled like crazy. The canoe chugged smoothly over the surface.

We were more than halfway across the lake when, behind us, the first Mega-Monster hit the water. He wouldn't be able to catch up with us before we reached the far shore. Of course, I didn't know what we would do then, but at least our chances were better than being stuck in the castle on the island.

"We're going to make it!" Mr. Williams exclaimed. Leah and Sandy cheered. I kept paddling as hard as ever.

And then—disaster struck.

30

We had made one terrible mistake. When we thought we could make it to the other side of the lake, we forgot that there might still be other Mega-Monsters around . . . ones that hadn't eaten the sardines! These Mega-Monsters wouldn't have grown to the size that the other ones had. They would be lurking in the water or in the forest. They could be anywhere!

And that's what happened.

Suddenly, right in front of the canoe, a Mega-Monster exploded from the surface! It looked just like the one we had seen in the swamp . . . covered with seaweed, with huge, red eyes and long, sharp claws. It was hideous.

I screamed. Then Leah screamed. Then Sandy. Even Mr. Williams let out a shout!

I tried to turn the canoe, but it was too late. The Mega-Monster reached out with his powerful, slimy arms and grabbed the boat.

"Let go!" I screamed, swinging the paddle at the beast. I bopped him on the head a couple times, but the creature didn't even feel it. I screamed at him again. "Let us go, you slimy warthog!"

I must have made him mad. The creature let out a bloodcurdling shriek, and twisted the boat sideways. The four of us plunged into the water. It was ice-cold, and it took my breath away. We immediately began to swim away from the beast.

"Sandy!" I sputtered, splashing the surface. "Sandy! You have to try! You have to! We don't have any other chance!"

She knew what I meant.

Sandy stopped swimming and shouted. "Mr. Williams! Grab my hand! Leah! Grab my other hand!"

Mr. Williams looked puzzled. "What are you going to—"

"Never mind now!" Sandy said, splashing in the water. "Just grab my hand. Rick . . . Grab Leah's hand. Everybody hang on tight!"

The Mega-Monster was only a few feet away.

"Hurry, Sandy!" Leah pleaded. "Hurry!"

We were all holding hands. Mr. Williams was looking around frantically, wondering what was going on.

And, with an angry snarl and a vicious swipe of his claw, the Mega-Monster attacked.

Suddenly, I could feel us beginning to rise up and out of the water!

"What on earth!" Mr. Williams exclaimed as we were lifted from the surface of the water.

"You're doing it, Sandy!" I cheered. "It's working!"

Below us, the Mega-Monster screamed out, reaching for us.

"Aaaaggghhh!!" I screamed. "He's got me!"

I kicked with all my might. The Mega-Monster had hold of my shoe with his claw. I kicked and kicked. Finally, my shoe came off, and we were free. Below me, the Mega-Monster popped the shoe into his mouth like it was candy.

"Those Nike's cost my dad fifty bucks!" I shouted down at the beast. "He's not going to be happy with you!"

After I said that, I felt a little silly. Oh well. We were safe. And I still had one shoe left, anyway.

Sandy continued to pull us higher and higher into the air. I held onto Leah's hand as tight as I could as we began to drift toward the shore.

"I . . . I can't go much longer," Sandy said. Her voice was shaky, and I could tell that she was having a hard time staying in the air.

"Just a little bit farther!" I shouted. The wind whipped at my face. "We're almost to the shore!"

I looked back at the island. The Mega-Monsters that had surrounded the castle were gone!

"Mr. Williams!" I shouted as we drifted through the air. "Look!"

Mr. Williams turned his head. "That's good!" he said. "I'll bet they've reached my laboratory!

They've reached my laboratory, and have eaten the sardines with the new potion! I'll bet they have shrunk and returned to their normal size!"

Suddenly, another Mega-Monster appeared in the water below us. It was yet another one that hadn't eaten the first batch of sardines. This one was smaller than the last one, but he was just as ugly and just as mean. I sure was glad we were up in the air!

Just then, we began to drift down toward the water!

"Sandy!" I cried, snapping my head around. "What's happening?!?!?"

"I . . . can't . . . go . . . any . . . more," she said. "I'm sorry! But I just can't fly any farther!"

Oh no! We were almost to shore!

And suddenly, we were falling. Sandy's power had faded, and the four of us were tumbling through the air toward the water . . . and toward the gaping jaws of a Mega-Monster.

31

The four of us screamed our heads off as we plummeted from the sky. In seconds, we would hit the surface of the water. In seconds, we would be attacked by the vicious Mega-Monster.

I felt helpless. There was nothing we could do now. For a while, I thought we would escape. I thought that we would get away.

Not anymore. It was the end of the line for us. There was no way we would be able to get away from the ravaging beast below us.

I hit the water first, and the surface became a

churning mass of arms and legs as Leah, Sandy, Mr. Williams and I splashed down. Several yards away, the slimy Mega-Monster let out another screech and attacked.

I spun in the water.

"Spread out!" I shouted. "Spread out so he doesn't know who to attack first!"

I crawled away, and Leah, Sandy, and Mr. Williams did the same.

It worked! The beast first chased after Mr. Williams, then started off after me! I kept swimming toward the shore, and then the creature went for Sandy! In the water, it couldn't move as fast as we could.

Suddenly, I found myself at the shore. I stood up. "Come on, Sandy!" I shouted. "You can make it!" I reached out and helped her up.

The two of us were safe on shore. Mr. Williams and Leah were still in the water, and the creature was trying to catch Mr. Williams.

"Hurry!" we screamed. "Hurry!"

Mr. Williams made it to shore, and we helped him out. Leah was right behind him . . . followed by the Mega-Monster.

"Leah!" we screamed. "He's right behind you!"

Leah was only a few feet from shore, but the monster was right behind her.

"Hurry!" Sandy screamed.

But it was too late. Just as Leah started to stand, the Mega-Monster reached out with his powerful arms. Leah shrieked as the horrible creature pulled her back into the water. She kicked and screamed, but it was no use. The Mega-Monster was too strong.

"Leah!" Sandy shouted. "You know what you have to do!"

I didn't know what Sandy meant. There was nothing Leah could do. In seconds, she would be devoured.

Mr. Williams was bewildered. He knew that there was nothing we could do.

"LEAH!" Sandy shrieked at the top of her lungs. "DO IT! DO IT NOW!"

"Do what?!?!" I asked. "What does she need to do? Maybe we can help!"

Sandy didn't answer me. The only thing we could do was watch as the awful creature held

Leah in his sharp claws . . . and pulled her beneath the surface of the water.

Leah was gone.

32

We all screamed. Water churned and boiled. There was nothing we could do.

I froze. Sandy froze. Mr. Williams froze.

Suddenly, there was movement on the surface, and I saw an arm raise up.

Except—

It wasn't a human arm. And it wasn't an arm from the Mega-Monster.

In the next instant, the water exploded, and not one, but *two* creatures emerged. The three of us jumped back from the shore and watched.

One of the creatures was the Mega-Monster, but the other . . . .

A giant spider! I couldn't believe what I was seeing!

"What is going on?!?!?!" I gasped.

"It's Leah!" Sandy exclaimed.

"What?!?!?" Mr. Williams and I both asked.

"Yes!" Sandy answered. "It's her! It really is!"

It can't be! I thought. The creature that was battling the Mega-Monster was a *spider!* It had eight, spiny legs and giant eyes. There was no way the creature could be human!

In the water, the two creatures battled one another. Water splashed and sprayed as the Mega-Monster and the enormous spider fought. The Mega-Monster was making weird screeching noises.

Suddenly, both creatures plunged beneath the surface. We waited on the shore for any sign of movement. Seconds ticked by. I didn't breathe.

Sandy was just about to speak when there was a sudden movement in the water.

It was the spider! The Mega-Monster was nowhere to be seen, and the spider began crawling out of the water.

I turned to run. There was no way I wanted to get captured by that thing!

"Wait!" Sandy shouted to me. "It's okay! It's Leah! It's *really* her!!"

I stopped running and turned back around. Even Mr. Williams had started to run, but he stopped when Sandy shouted.

The giant spider spread its long, tree-sized legs and pulled itself out of the water. It was the most bizarre creature I had ever seen in my life.

Well, *almost.* The Mega-Monsters were probably stranger.

And what happened next was something so strange, so weird, that I thought I was going to faint.

33

The spider began to twist and turn. *It was changing! It was turning into something!*

The creature began to shrink, and as I watched, it was becoming more—

human!

Sandy was right! I didn't know how, but Leah had turned into a spider . . . and now she was changing back into a human!

Talk about *freaky!*

Mr. Williams couldn't believe what he was seeing, either. He stood frozen, his mouth open, watching as the strange creature went through an eerie metamorphosis. In just a few seconds, the spider had changed back into a human.

The spider was Leah!

"H . . . how . . . how did you—" I stammered.

Leah just smiled. "I'm an arachno-sapien," she replied. "I'm half-human, half-spider."

A what? Impossible. I'd never heard of such a thing.

Yet, I had seen it with my own eyes. I had watched Leah change from a spider into a human.

"It's a long story," she said. "I'll tell you about it later."

I just shook my head. I had met two new friends at camp. One of them could fly, and the other one could turn into a giant spider. On top of that, I'd just had the most bizarre adventure that I'd ever had in my life.

Mr. Williams didn't say a thing. I could tell he was shocked, but we'd all been through a lot in just the past hour.

"Come on," he said. "Let's get back to camp. There are probably people looking for you already."

Mr. Williams led the way. We followed the shore of the lake, and then began walking through the thick forest. Mr. Williams said that, although he usually used his helicopter, he knew which direction the camp was.

It was tough going through the woods. There was no trail at all, so we had to push branches away as we walked.

And the farther we got from the lake, the better the weather became. Soon, the sky was blue and the sun was shining. Birds sang in the trees. We were safe. We were safe, and we were on our way back to camp. All of the Mega-Monsters were gone.

At least, I *thought* they were gone.

We were about to find out differently.

34

We had been walking for about twenty minutes when all of a sudden, Mr. Williams stopped. He held his hand up, and Sandy, Leah, and I stopped walking. We listened.

The forest seemed eerily quiet. I hadn't noticed it, but all of the birds had stopped singing. The only thing I heard was a fly as it buzzed past my head.

Suddenly, a loud shriek boomed through the forest, and I knew instantly what it was.

A Mega-Monster.

And judging from how close the sound was, the Mega-Monster couldn't be far.

We moved our heads slowly, searching the forest, but we didn't see anything. Wherever the beast was, we couldn't see him.

"Let's keep moving," Mr. Williams said. He placed his fingers to his lips. *"We'll go real slow and as quiet as we can."*

We moved slowly, but no matter how hard we tried, it was difficult to stop branches and twigs from snapping beneath our feet. I kept glancing nervously around, wary of the Mega-Monster that was lurking nearby.

"Can't you just turn into a spider again?" I whispered to Leah.

"Yes, if I have enough time," she answered quietly. *"But it will be hard with all of these branches."*

It was almost impossible to move without making any noise. Mr. Williams raised his hand again to halt us, and we stopped. We all looked around, listening. Maybe the Mega-Monster had decided not to attack. Maybe we were out of danger.

But we weren't going to take any chances.

We started moving again, still walking slowly through the brush. After a few minutes, my nervousness went away. I was sure the Mega-Monster had picked up the scent of the sardines, and was on his way to the lake.

The day was now sunny and bright again. It was very different than the weather that Mr. Williams controlled around his island and lake and castle!

"Man," I said in a normal voice. "For a while, I didn't think we were going to make it out alive."

"Me too," Sandy chimed in. "I'm sure glad we're almost back to the camp."

"We're not there yet," Mr. Williams said. His voice was nervous. I looked around, but I didn't see anything. No Mega-Monster hiding behind a tree or in the brush.

So when we suddenly heard a scream from above, the four of us freaked. My head snapped up, and I knew that there was no way we were going to make it back now.

It was a Mega-Monster! He had been hiding in the top of a tree! His color made him blend in perfectly.

We only had a split-instant of warning before he leapt from the branch. Suddenly, he was falling, his huge arms outstretched, his mouth full of fangs wide open. He let out a terrible shriek.

Oh no! He was going to land right on top of us!

35

We didn't have time to get out of the way. The ugly beast came crashing down right on top of us! I was pounded into the ground so hard that the wind was knocked from me.

I struggled to get up, but the awful beast was too heavy. I couldn't even move.

And man . . . did he *stink!* He smelled awful! This guy needed a bath! The Mega-Monster was wet and slimy and I gasped as his terrible odor stung my nostrils.

Finally, the creature shrieked and got to his

feet. I immediately jumped up. Sandy was beside me, and I grabbed her hand and pulled.

"Come on!" I said.

We ran into the bushes. Behind us, Mr. Williams was telling Leah to run, to get away.

But Leah wasn't moving . . . *or was she?*

The Mega-Monster reached out to grab Leah, but she jumped back.

She was moving, alright. She was changing. *She was changing into a spider!*

It was unbelievable. I watched as she grew long, dark legs. She became larger, and her color changed as she morphed into a spider. If I hadn't seen it with my own eyes, I wouldn't have believed it.

As the Mega-Monster attacked, Leah climbed back and easily was able to get away.

But she did more than that.

With one of her powerful, long legs, she reached out and grabbed the Mega-Monster. Then she grabbed the creature with another one of her legs. The Mega-Monster growled and struggled to get away, but Leah was too strong.

Using her other legs, she reached up and

pulled herself into a tree. She was still clinging tightly to the Mega-Monster with her other two legs.

Then, something even stranger happened.

Leah began to spin the Mega-Monster around. The beast tried to get away, but Leah held tightly with her two powerful legs. White string began to fly all over the place, covering the Mega-Monster.

Wait a minute! I thought. *That's not string! That's webbing! Leah was wrapping up the monster in a web!*

It really was cool to see. The Mega-Monster continued to try and break free, but Leah kept spinning the beast around faster and faster. She was using four legs now, hanging tightly from the branch with her remaining four legs. Shiny white webbing wrapped tightly around the head and shoulders of the Mega-Monster. Soon, the creature couldn't move at all. Leah spun the monster around and around until it was completely wrapped in a silky cocoon.

"Alright Leah!" I shouted, thrusting my fist into the air. Sandy clapped her hands together. Mr. Williams just stared, wide eyed, in complete disbelief.

Leah pulled the Mega-Monster into the tree, and began wrapping the giant cocoon to a branch high in the air. When she was sure that the creature was secure, she climbed down the tree and began to change back into her human form. In only a few seconds, she was a human again.

"Can you show me how to do that?" I asked. I thought it would be really cool if I could change into a spider! Man, I could freak out my friends really good!

"I'm afraid it's not possible," Leah said. She smiled. "Not unless you're an arachno-sapien like me."

Rats. I really thought it would be great to change into a spider when I wanted to.

We continued walking. Finally, we found the trail that led back to camp.

"You're on your own from here," Mr. Williams said.

"You're not coming with us?" I asked. Mr. Williams shook his head.

"No," he said. "There is much to do at my laboratory. You three need to return to camp. I'll be fine. Now that I've discovered the serum that will change the animals back to their original sizes, I'll be quite busy for a while. Thank you all so much for your help." He shook hands with us, then turned and began trudging through the forest. He was gone, as simple as that.

It didn't take us long to reach the camp. Surprisingly, we were only five minutes late for the next activity. Our patrol leader asked us where we had been, and how half of my shirt had been ripped away.

"You wouldn't believe it," I answered, shaking my head. "You just wouldn't believe it."

36

We decided that it would be better not to tell anyone about the bizarre events that we'd experienced this day. In the first place, we were sure that no one would believe us. Secondly, we didn't want to give away Mr. Williams's secret. Then everyone would know where his castle was.

Besides . . . Sandy and Leah didn't want anyone to know about their secrets, either.

Later that night, around the campfire, everyone told spooky stories and strange tales. I kept looking over at Sandy and Leah, and they smiled back at me. We knew that the story that we could tell would be better than any others that we'd heard.

There were a bunch of kids from Michigan that said, over the past year, some really creepy things had happened to them. A girl named Alex from the city of Petoskey told a story about her house being haunted. She said that it is still haunted to this very day.

Another kid named Matt Sorenson told a story about a giant, hairy beast that he accidentally created. It ravaged Traverse City until he and his friend John and a curious magician were able to send it back to where it belonged.

There were more stories, too.

A kid from Alpena, Mark Blackburn, told a story about aliens from outer space that attacked, and how he and his friend had fended them off. A girl from Gaylord named Corky MacArthur talked about real gargoyles in her town. And a girl name Kayleigh Fisher related a horrifying story about weird clowns that had taken over the carnival in Kalamazoo.

Of course, no one believed any of the stories.

We knew that they were just making them up.

Or were they?

It was getting late, and the fire was dying down. Orange embers glowed, and the yellow flames dwindled down to tiny tongues. Soon, the flames were gone, leaving only a pile of orange and black coals.

"Okay Wolf Patrol," Mr. Leonard said. "Time to pack it up for the night."

We all stood up, and other patrols did the same. Everyone began returning to their cabins.

I saw Leah walking away, and I walked up to her.

"Hey," I said quietly. "You've got to tell me how you do that spider-thing," I said.

Leah smiled. "Well, it's kind of a long story," she replied. "How about tomorrow? After breakfast?"

"Promise?" I asked.

"Promise," Leah agreed.

Next morning, I met Leah and Sandy for breakfast in the huge mess hall. The room was filled with talking and laughter as we ate.

"You, too," I said, looking at Sandy.

"Me, too, what?" Sandy replied, frowning.

"I want to hear your story," I said. "I want to know more about how you found that stone that makes you fly."

She smiled, and began her strange tale about a really weird adventure she and her brother had on Mackinac Island. I think my mouth hung open the entire time she was talking.

When she finished, it was time to clean up our breakfast trays and silverware. We had an hour before our first activity, which would be a hike around the camp.

"Now," I said to Leah, "I want to hear *your* story."

"Okay," she replied. "Let's go outside and I'll tell you everything."

Nearly an hour later, Leah had finished.

"You don't believe me?" Leah asked, noticing my look of disbelief.

"Yes, I believe you," I answered, bobbing my head. "I saw you change into a spider, so I know that you're not trying to fool me. The crazy thing is ... well ... around the campfire last night. Did you hear all of those stories about those kids from Michigan?"

Leah nodded.

"I wonder ... I wonder if those things really happened. I wonder if they weren't making those stories up."

Leah shook her head. "I don't know, Rick," she replied. "But the world can be a very strange place."

She's right about that, I thought. *The world sure can be a pretty strange – and weird – place.*

"Come on," Leah said. She stood up. "It's time for our hike."

We walked toward the flag pole and met up with the rest of our patrol, and we followed Mr. Leonard down trails that led around the camp. He pointed out various trees and animals, and we even saw a bald eagle high in the air.

But I couldn't get my mind off the things that had happened yesterday, and the things that Leah and Sandy had told me today.

Some things are just too strange to

understand.

But there was one strange story that I was about to hear that was even more bizarre than anything else I'd ever heard or experienced, and it was told to me by a girl in one of the other patrols.

We had finished our hike, and I had gone to the camp store to buy a couple candy bars. I unwrapped one and began eating as I walked down to the lake.

A girl was sitting on the dock. She was all alone, staring out over the water. I had seen her a few times over the past few days. She seemed quiet and maybe a little shy.

"Hi," I said, walking onto the dock. "You want one?" I held out my remaining candy bar.

"No, thanks," she said. "Thank you for asking."

She turned away and continued gazing out over the lake, and I couldn't help but notice that she seemed worried.

"My name is Rick Owens," I said.

She glanced up at me. She looked a little frightened.

"I'm Danielle," she said. "Danielle Reed."

"What's wrong?" I asked, sitting down next to her.

She didn't answer right away, but rather, continued looking over the water. I hoped that I hadn't made her mad or anything.

Finally, she spoke.

"We have to go home tomorrow," Danielle said. "Tomorrow is our last day."

"You're going to miss Camp Willow?" I asked.

"Well, yeah," she replied. "But there's more to it than that. I'm from Ohio."

I've been to Ohio before. It's a state that borders Michigan to the south.

"You don't like Ohio?" I asked.

She shook her head. "No, that's not it at all. I *love* Ohio. I've lived there all my life. It's great. It's the ogres I can do without."

Huh? I thought. *What was she talking about?*

"I don't understand," I said. "What's an 'ogre'?"

"Ogres are weird creatures. They are bigger than you and I, and they have horrible teeth and pointy ears and noses. They are horrible looking."

"Yeah?" I said. "But what about them?"

And Danielle told me a story that haunts me to this very day . . . .

Next:

**#2: Ogres
of
Ohio**

**Continue on for
a FREE preview!**

"Well Danielle . . . what do you think?"

I almost didn't hear my dad ask the question. I was looking out the rain-streaked car window, staring up at the big, two-story house that was now our home.

"It's . . . it's huge," I replied, trying not to sound nervous.

But I was. I was really nervous. There was something about the house that was just . . .

Creepy.

"I think you'll like it here," Mom said. "The

rooms are big, and there is a fireplace on both floors."

Through the rain, the dark house looked cold and uninviting.

"It looks kind of lonely," I said.

"That's because no one has lived here in a while," Dad said, turning the key and shutting off the car engine. "It needs someone like us to take care of it. In a few months from now, we'll have flowers all around. The lawn will be fresh and green, and it will look like a home. Our home."

Dad was wrong, of course. The house wouldn't be a home.

It would be a nightmare.

We just didn't know it yet.

Our move from Columbus, Ohio, to Sandusky, Ohio, happened pretty fast. Dad's company transferred him, and we needed to find a new home fast. I knew I was going to miss my friends in Columbus, but I was pretty excited to move. Sandusky is a city in northern Ohio, and our home was only a few miles from Lake Erie, one of the Great Lakes.

But best of all, Sandusky is home to a place called Cedar Point. It's a really cool amusement park with awesome roller coasters and rides. We went there once on a class field trip, and when my dad told me that we would be moving to Sandusky, I couldn't believe it! I'd be living only a few miles from Cedar Point!

Too cool.

Walking inside our new home for the first time was like walking into a cave. The windows had been boarded up, so everything was very dark. The floors were wood, and my wet sneakers squeaked as I walked down the hall.

"You can pick any room upstairs," Dad said. "Whichever one you want."

Awesome! My dorky brother was spending the week at grandma and grandpa's, so I got to pick the best room first!

I flipped a light switch in the hall and nothing happened. I tried it again.

Still nothing.

"Dad," I called out. "The lights don't work."

"The power is still shut off," he said. "The

electric company will be out later today to turn it on. Hang on a sec."

His heavy footsteps echoed down the hall, and suddenly he appeared around a corner. He was carrying a flashlight.

"Take this," he said, handing me the light. "And be careful. All of the windows upstairs are boarded up, so it will be pretty dark."

"Don't stay up there long, Danielle," Mom called out from the kitchen. "We have a lot of unpacking to do."

Dad walked away, and his footsteps faded down the hall. I looked up at the dark, winding staircase, sweeping the flashlight beam over the steps. Outside, thunder cracked.

I took one step up, then another. One more.

Another jolt of thunder exploded outside as I took another step. Ten more steps and I would be on the second floor.

I kept going, unaware of the awful things that were going to happen to me.

For the record, I don't get spooked easily. My brother Derek, who is ten, is always trying to freak me out in some way or another, so I'm always on the lookout for his silly pranks.

But Derek was at grandma and grandpa's for the rest of the week, and I shouldn't have to worry about his goofy antics.

So when I saw the strip of light coming from beneath one of the bedroom doors, I knew that it wasn't my brother playing a joke on me.

How can that be? I thought, staring at the light coming from beneath one of the closed bedroom doors. It glowed brightly, like there was a light on inside.

But that was impossible. Dad said there was no electricity in the house, and we wouldn't have any power until later in the day.

How could a light be on?

Just to be sure, I reached out and flipped a light switch on the wall.

Nothing. The staircase remained dark.

And the glowing bar below the bedroom door was as bright as ever.

There has to be some reason for the light, I thought. *Maybe the bedroom window inside that room isn't boarded up, and it's letting in light from outside.*

No, that couldn't be it. It was too cloudy and rainy outside. The light coming from below the bedroom door had a yellow cast to it, like it was coming from a lamp or a ceiling light.

Regardless, there had to be *some* reason.

I walked slowly toward the door, not making a sound. Another crash of thunder boomed, and a gust of wind howled and groaned like a snarling lion. I could hear rain on the roof, and rain hitting the side of the house.

When I was right in front of the door, I stopped. I clicked off the flashlight.

At my feet, the glowing light from beneath the door was bright enough to illuminate my sneakers.

I leaned toward the door, listening for any movement. I heard nothing.

Slowly, ever so slowly, I reached out and grasped the doorknob. It was metal, and it felt cold in my hand.

I turned it. It jiggled a little bit, and then there was a light *thunk*. I pushed the door.

Instantly, the light went out! I didn't even have time to see where it had come from!

The door squeaked as it swung open, exposing nothing but darkness.

I quickly turned on the flashlight Dad had given me. The beam penetrated the darkness like a laser beam, and I swept it across the dark room.

There was nothing there.

That was kind of freaky. I know that I had

seen a light coming from beneath the door.

I *knew* it.

Yet, behind the door, there was nothing but inky blackness.

I moved the beam back and forth through the room.

It was totally empty. There was nothing in the room at all.

I reached around the wall and fumbled for the light, switch. I found it, and clicked it up and down several times.

No lights came on. Except for the flashlight beam, the room remained cloaked in darkness.

I reached out and grasped the doorknob, slowly pulling the door closed. Its hinges squeaked as the door swung toward me, and made a loud click as it shut.

At that point, I was about to turn and leave. Maybe I just *thought* that I had seen a light. Maybe it was just my imagination.

But the moment the door clicked shut, I knew that I hadn't imagined the light.

Because it had returned.

At my feet, a light from beneath the door

blinked on, once again illuminating my sneakers.

I immediately took a giant step back.

There was no mistake about it. There was a light on in that room. I was seeing it with my own eyes.

And what made me decide to open that door again, I'll never know. But I'll tell you this: what was about to happen would be the strangest — and scariest — thing that would ever happen to me in my whole entire life.

My heart jackhammered in my chest.

Pound-pound-pound-pound-pound . . . .

Where was that light coming from?

I slowly dropped down on my hands and knees, being careful not to bang the flashlight on the hard floor. I leaned over until my cheek touched the cold floor.

I peered beneath the door.

Now I was *certain* that there was a light on. Under the crack of the door, I could see the floor inside the room. I could see a tiny portion of the wall on the other side of the room.

There was no mistake. I hadn't been imagining things.

There was a light on in the bedroom.

I remained motionless, staring under the bedroom door through the thin strip of light. My mind raced.

Where could that light be coming from? I thought.

Thunder clapped outside and I jumped. The noise had surprised me.

I stood up slowly, quietly, all the while staring down at the thin strip of light that came from beneath the door.

Grasping the flashlight tightly, I clicked it on and took a step forward. I held my breath, reached out, and grasped the doorknob.

I waited there a moment, nervously looking at the light at my feet. Then I looked at my hand around the knob, then glanced back down at the bottom of the door.

The light was still on.

I took a deep breath, preparing myself. After all, I was twelve. I'm not afraid of a strange light in a bedroom.

Am I?

I guess at the time, I wasn't sure. That's why I was hesitating.

I took another breath, held it, turned the knob quickly, and threw the door open. I pushed it and let it go. It spun on its hinges and smacked into the wall with a crash.

But the light . . . .

What happened next is difficult to describe. There was a light in the bedroom, alright—but it didn't seem to be coming from anywhere! It was like a mist that swarmed around the room. When the door opened, the weird light-mist swirled like smoke and began seeping through the cracks of a boarded-up window, like it was trying to hide!

I did nothing but stare. I had never seen anything like this before in my entire life.

Within seconds, the light was gone, seeping through the cracks in the boards like water.

The room was dark once again!

I've seen television shows that investigate strange things that happen to people and places. Most of what I've seen can usually be explained by something or another. I've read books about odd things that happen without explanation.

That's how I felt right now. Like this was something out of a book.

Only it was real. It had happened to me. I had watched the light slither about the room and vanish like mist.

But hang on a minute.

I trained the flashlight beam at the boarded-up window, and for the first time, I realized that I was shaking in my shoes. The flashlight trembled in my hand, and my knees shook.

Alright, Danielle, I ordered myself. *Get hold of yourself. There's a simple explanation for this.*

I held the light in one spot, and the bright white spot lit up the boards that had been affixed to the wall.

Wait a minute, I thought. *That's not a window after all.*

It was true. Now that I took a closer look, the boards were nailed from the floor to the ceiling. On the other wall, where more boards were affixed, they covered only enough space to fill the window.

But here, where I had watched the light

disappear, the boards seemed to cover much more than a window.

The boards were covering up a door.

Why would someone board up a door? I wondered. *Where did it lead to? Was it a door that led downstairs? Or outside?*

I moved the beam of light around, exposing the boards and the far wall.

It was a door, I was certain. Behind those boards was a door.

Why?

I've always been curious. I'm always trying to find out how things work, why things work, and why things do what they do. I guess I just have a curious mind.

A curious mind that gets me into trouble sometimes. I can't help it, though. I just need to have answers.

I'm just curious, that's all.

There's a saying that my brother is always repeating. He says *'curiosity killed the cat, Danielle. Curiosity killed the cat.'*

But I can't help it. I'm just curious. I like to know things.

And my curiosity about the strange, boarded-up door was about to land me in *big* trouble.

Why I didn't go and get my mom and dad I'll never know. Maybe I just wanted to investigate the door myself.

Whatever the reason, I found myself tip-toeing slowly across the bedroom floor, the white splotch of light trained on the wall before me.

Outside, the wind cried. Thunder rumbled in the distance, and the rain dripped off the roof. It sounded like the storm might be passing.

I stopped a few inches before the wall. The

flashlight beam lit up the boards, and, sure enough, I was right.

There *was* a door boarded up. I could see the wood through the cracks of the boards.

Why would someone board up a door? I thought once again. *To keep people out? Why?*

I reached out slowly, and my brother's words echoed in my head.

Curiosity killed the cat, Danielle. Curiosity killed the cat.

My finger touched one of the boards. It was old and dry. I felt the edge of it and began to pry it with my fingers. It took some work, but after a minute or two I was able to wiggle the board loose. In another minute I had succeeded in grasping it with my hand and pulling it from the wall.

I pulled the board away, set it aside on the floor, and went to work at another board. It, too, required some work, but after a few minutes I was able to pull it free. The board came away, and I placed it on the floor next to the other one.

Curiosity killed the cat, Danielle. Curiosity killed the cat.

I grasped another board. This one came away easy, and I placed it on the floor next to the other two.

Soon, all of the boards had been pulled away, exposing a large, wood door. The handle had been broken off. Whoever had closed up the door really wanted to keep people out.

I tried to fit my fingers around the edge of the door to pry it open.

No luck. There wasn't enough room to get fingers in the crack between the door and the frame. I tried to grab hold of the broken doorknob, but that didn't work, either.

I shined the light all around the door. Besides the fact that it had been boarded-up and had a broken doorknob, it looked like any other wood door.

But in the bright light, I saw something else.

Scratch marks.

On the face of the door were long, thin scratch marks, like someone had carved on the door with a knife.

I leaned closer, bringing the light near the door.

No, not scratch marks, I thought. *Letters. There's something written on this door!*

I leaned closer still to make out the strange markings.

"*Danger,*" I whispered, reading the words quietly. "*Do not open door. Or else . . .*"

I drew back.

Or else *what?* The warning abruptly stopped with a long scratch that went all the way down the door. It looked like someone had tried to finish writing something, but couldn't.

Now I was *really* curious. Why would someone write such a thing? It was only a door. Maybe it went to a closet or another room. Or maybe it didn't go anywhere. I wondered if Dad and Mom had seen the door when they came to look at the house before they bought it.

I stared at the words carved into the door. It looked like someone had used a small knife to inscribe the warning. The scratches weren't very deep, and if you didn't look close, you wouldn't even be able to see them.

I was standing in front of the door, wondering what and why someone would go through the trouble to write something on the door, then board it up . . . when all of a sudden I knew what had made the words in the wood.

Except, I realized it too late—because in the next instant I could feel sharp fingernails clawing into my back.

5

The sharp claws dug into my back, and I spun and screamed at the same time. I whirled and flung myself against the wall, shining the light at my attacker.

"YOU!" I screamed.

In the flashlight beam, Derek looked back at me, smirking. He was holding a fake claw hand.

"See what Grandpa got me for my birthday?" he said, holding the plastic hand up for me to see. It was gross. It looked like a creepy monster's hand, with fake fur and long, sharp nails.

"You just about scared me to death!" I scolded.

"Maybe I can do better next time," he said smartly.

"What are you doing here, anyway?" I asked. "You're supposed to be at Grandma and Grandpa's house in Toledo all week."

"They wanted to come and see our new house. Besides . . . I haven't even seen it myself."

"Well, you didn't need to sneak up on me like you did!"

"Why?" he asked, looking over my shoulder at the dark wall and closed door. "Are you doing something you shouldn't be?"

"No," I replied sharply. "I'm not. I was just—"

What, exactly, was I doing? I wondered.

"I was just curious, that's all," I finished.

"Looks like you're wrecking our new house, if you ask me," Derek replied. Even with the flashlight beam trained on him, he could see the pile of boards on the floor behind me.

He pointed to the door. "Where does that

go?" he asked.

"I don't know," I replied, turning to face the door. "I was trying to get it open. Someone had boarded it up. And here—"

I reached out and dragged a finger over the scratched letters. "Someone wrote this in the wood."

Derek stepped next to me and leaned toward the door, reading the words out loud.

"Danger. Do not open door. Or else." He stopped reading and faced me. "Or else what?"

"You've got me," I said, shrugging. "I was just trying to figure that out when you came up and scared me."

"I did a good job, didn't I?" he sneered, holding up the fake hand.

I punched him in the shoulder. Not hard, but hard enough. He winced, but he kept looking at the door.

"Maybe it's just a closet," he said.

"But why would someone board it up?" I asked. "And why would they scratch a warning in the door?"

"Beats me," Derek said. He turned to walk

away.

"You're not even curious to know what is behind it?" I asked.

"Nope," he replied, shaking his head. "I've got better things to do than waste my day staring at some door. It was probably someone's idea as a joke."

Derek is right, I thought. *Whoever lived here before probably did this as a joke.*

I turned to follow my brother out of the bedroom. He was walking down the hall, and I had just stepped out of the room when I heard a creak.

Then another.

I turned, flashed the light into the room we had come from . . . and my blood ran cold.

"Derek!" I whispered. *"Look!"*

Derek was just about to go into another bedroom when he turned around and walked back to where I was standing. He looked into the room.

The door that I had discover . . . the one that I had pulled the boards from . . . *was open!*

"D . . . did you d . . . do that?" Derek

stammered.

"How could I do it?" I replied. "I was standing right here!"

But it wasn't the open door that made us gasp in horror — it was what was beyond the door that made Derek and I tremble with fear.

AMERICA'S #1 SERIES FOR MAXIMUM CHILLS!

Want to read Sandy Johnson's story? Pick up

MICHIGAN CHILLERS #1: Mayhem on Mackinac Island

and read Leah Warner's story in

MICHIGAN CHILLERS #9: Sinister Spiders of Saginaw

and be sure to visit www.americanchillers.com to read
sample chapters on-line for FREE!

ABOUT THE AUTHOR

nnathan Rand is the author of more than 65 books, with well
er 4 million copies in print. Series include **AMERICAN**
HILLERS, MICHIGAN CHILLERS, FREDDIE
ERNORTNER, FEARLESS FIRST GRADER, and **THE**
DVENTURE CLUB. He's also co-authored a novel for teens
ith Christopher Knight) entitled **PANDEMIA**. When not trav-
ng, Rand lives in northern Michigan with his wife and three
gs. He is also the only author in the world to have a store that
lls only his works: **CHILLERMANIA!** is located in Indian
ver, Michigan. Johnathan Rand is not always at the store, but he
s been known to drop by frequently. Find out more at:

www.americanchillers.com

Join the official

AMERICAN

CHILLERS

FAN CLUB!

Visit www.americanchillers.com for details!

Johnathan Rand travels internationally for school visits and book signings! For booking information, call:

1 (231) 238-0338!

All AudioCraft books are proudly printed, bound, and manufactured in the United States of America, utilizing American resources, labor, and materials.

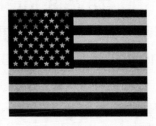

USA